True Romance

Helen Zahavi

Secker & Warburg
London

First published in Great Britain in 1994
by Martin Secker & Warburg Limited,
an imprint of Reed Consumer Books Limited,
Michelin House, 81 Fulham Road, London SW3 6RB
and Auckland, Melbourne, Singapore and Toronto

A CIP catalogue record for this book
is available from the British Library
ISBN 0 436 20207 7

Printed and bound in Great Britain
by Clays Ltd, St Ives plc.

for N

1

There were three of them, in all, if one counted very carefully. Him and him and her. A trinity of persons of a carnal disposition.

Some might say the one from overseas, she whose passport had expired, the female of the little group, the one endowed with mammaries, was actually the cause of what ensued, the spark and catalyst of all that was to follow. But that would be too harsh a view, a shade too unforgiving, of one whose single and abiding vice was her sweet, obliging nature.

In any case, she came to them by chance. She landed at their feet without quite knowing why. She could have chosen somewhere else. Anywhere, in fact, that wasn't where she was. She even might have stayed, she never would have left, had she felt more cherished by the natives.

But the natives hadn't wanted her. They'd been getting rather restless, and it meant she had to go. (When natives want to get you out, you often have to go.)

It was only the burning that made her leave. She'd been contented, up till then, though not ecstatic. She'd stayed inside her concrete space, and listened to the radio, and lived her undemanding life, but the burning meant she had to go. She wasn't one to whine, but she couldn't bear the thought of being burnt. She'd always had this ego thing, this self-indulgent sense of who she was, and she didn't want to roast, if she could possibly avoid it. She didn't want her tender flesh to blacken in the flames, nor did she want to be there when they stormed her block of flats. Confrontations, and other aggravations, were not, alas, her cup of tea.

So when she met a man who said he'd take her to the coast – a slim and charming man, of muscular dimensions – she readily agreed. He swore he'd see her safely right across the water. (And furthermore for free, he added, not without a hint of modest pride.) He wrapped her in his overcoat, and hid her in the cabin of his lorry, feeding her with scrambled eggs and wholebran toast from the ferry cafeteria. My treat, he said, and brushed away her thanks.

Secreting her beneath his legs, he drove ashore at Harwich, and Customs waved him through without a murmur. Once clear and on the road again, she sat beside him, prim and grateful, silent on the plastic seat. She liked to watch his forearms at the wheel. Being of a pure and simple nature, she was moved by manly forearms on a leather-covered wheel.

But what impressed her most, the aspect of her saviour that touched her most profoundly, was the way he quoted from the classics. He seemed to know whole chunks and slabs of verse, he'd memorised entire and perfect passages. Reams of it, he knew, and prose to break your heart, pumping from his mouth in rhythmic bursts of erudition. A self-taught man, he promised her, can always be relied on.

They rolled through Essex, the happy pair, exchanging mild asides, and watched the sunlight flicker through the trees. With polite and total lack of interest, he didn't ask her where she came from, he never questioned why she'd left. He didn't seem to wonder what had made her so combustible. A gentleman, she realised. He'd rather not be thought intrusive. He felt it better not to probe. Whatever, she was grateful. His sensitivity appealed.

He detoured down the A13, went past the Hornchurch marshes, turned off at Castle

Green, and then the self-taught man applied the brakes and pulled onto the verge.

'Is this London?'

'More or less,' he said. 'Near enough,' he added. 'The locals call it Dagenham.'

He came around the front, and held her by the arm, and helped her down the metal steps. She thought it rather kind of him, to consider her like that. It showed a rare imagination, to know she had to stretch her legs, to understand her need for air upon her skin. For she was of a type that has to spread its limbs, from time to time, a type quite disinclined to stay cooped up too long. A type quite partial to the random kindnesses of strangers. So she let him take her by the hand, and lead her down the slope. Conscious that her passport had expired, the unprotesting alien, the displaced person from abroad, let him lead her down the steep and grassy slope.

Then there came a blank, an absence of sensation, a sudden comprehension that you couldn't gorge yourself, you couldn't stuff yourself with wholebran toast, and scrambled egg, without regretting it much later. You couldn't tend to be inflammable, and hitch a ride with someone erudite, and let him pay for breakfast on the ferry, and not expect to have him pull onto the verge, and help you down the metal

4

steps, and make you kiss the fertile earth of Dagenham.

When he'd finished being kind to her, he wiped himself, and wished her all the best. Then he buttoned what was open, and climbed back in the cab. He wound the window down. It was her last and final sighting of his gentle, sated face.

'So long,' he said. 'Be seeing you.'

Ignition on, and into first. The hiss as he released the brakes.

'Be careful, next time. Taking lifts.'

And he waved a cheery cheerio, and eased on to the road, and drove away.

So that, in short, was her. That was how she brought herself to England. By such a route, in such a way, the nomad from across the sea, that fragrant little vagrant, the menstruating section of the tight and clammy troika, had finished up quite near her future friends.

She doubtless would have claimed her motives were the highest, for like many blessed with ovaries, like many of the female inclination, all she ever wanted was a bit of ready cash, a heap of printed paper she could call her very own. It was a pure, untainted yearning for her private share of paradise. But what she wanted wasn't what she got.

What she got was something else entirely.

Initially, she found a well-bred man called Max. And then she found another man called Bruno. And then she found she had them both, she found that they could operate in tandem, she found that they were capable of being kind together.

(She never kept the money. She had it, for an hour or two, but then she lost it. They took it from her, plucked it from her sticky grasp, and bent her down, and taught her not to steal. A salutary lesson, and she learnt it very well.)

But all this came much later, once they'd interacted to the full, then let her out to see how she would manage. It happened somewhat later in their special kind of bonding, once the boys accepted that she'd have to earn her keep. First she had to find her feet. She had to navigate a route across the capital, stumble through the rain-washed streets and try to look like she belonged.

Another type of woman, one more suited to privation, might have found a furnished room, or felt a sudden urge to take a job. But she didn't have the patience. She had different kinds of urges.

She was young, and poor and needy. Her neediness was palpable: she needed someone rich. How fortunate, therefore, how vastly providential, that God created Max.

2

'I'm sure you'll settle in,' he said, paying off the taxi-driver. He took the change and flicked his wallet shut.

'Just give it time.'

The reassuring words, the breath against her face.

'A day or two, perhaps.'

She noted that he gave a generous tip. She didn't like to pry, but she always noticed things like that. She cut them out and filed them in her head, these coded indications of the hidden man within. She knew a man prepared to tip so lavishly, a man so free with his estate, might lift her from her current destitution, would appreciate her very many appetites.

'You're standing in one of the better parts of

town,' he said, 'one of the choicer areas. So you can't complain, you really can't.'

He waved a hand towards the sluggish water that sucked and flowed a yard or two behind them.

'Not quite Belgravia, of course.'

The slightest hint of mild regret.

'But then where is, one often asks oneself.'

She observed the line of mansion houses, white and brilliant in the sun, a drawn-out symphony of balustrades, and porticos, and other signs of affluence. Perfection, to her newly-opened, uncomplaining eyes.

The whiff, she could ignore. The faint, familiar odour barely registered. It was coming from the water, a slightly acrid, vaguely yellow, kind of smell. But the buildings, she enthused. The beauty of the buildings.

'They look quite glorious,' she said. 'So creamy-white.'

'I take your point, but we who live here, we who have the great good luck to occupy this neighbourhood, prefer to call them smegma-white. Between ourselves, if you follow me. *Entre nous*, I mean.'

She nibbled shyly at the word, this fresh and unknown smegma-word. She held it in her mouth and touched it with her tongue. She was sure she'd grow to like this man. In time, she felt, they'd bond.

(She couldn't have imagined – and Max had half-forgotten – that he'd also come from somewhere else, he'd also been a greener in the land. But he'd changed his name, rebuilt himself, and prospered rather splendidly, so it hardly seemed appropriate to mention it.)

The five stone steps she had to climb to reach his lacquered door, the ascent she made, minor as it was, induced in her an appropriate sense of humility, an opaque awareness that he would always be, in every way, above her. She watched him moving on ahead: the well-cut suit, the shoulder-blades, the shaven neck. So vain, he looked. So quietly vicious. To think she'd found a man like that, in a house like this. Her little bit of rough, in Little Venice.

Once inside the hall – or vestibule, so grand it was – she nearly fainted from the scent, she almost buckled at the knee. Such an odour of delight, a smell of inch-thick carpeting and polished wood and total lack of doubt. A concentrated money-smell. Stuffing both her nostrils with the unaccustomed reek, inhaling with abandon, she let him take her coat. (Not just rich, she thought, approvingly. But manners, too.)

Being partial to civility, she warmed to him,

she liquefied, and a single pearl, a drop of molten heat, came slowly trickling out.

'I'm glad you came,' he said. 'Grateful that you trusted me. I thought you might, indeed hoped you would, but one couldn't be quite sure. Not absolutely positive. Females being known for their capriciousness.'

He opened a panelled door, and ushered her politely through. The huge and sun-filled drawing room, of a stark, uncluttered grace, overlooked the canal below. Three floor-to-ceiling windows, flanked by wooden shutters, opened out on to a crescent balcony. Mine, she thought, triumphantly. All mine.

She watched him move towards a table by the wall, and hover, for a moment, as he picked between the bottles.

'I assume you drink,' he said. 'I take it you imbibe, from time to time.'

He poured a stream of colourless liquid into a pair of crystal glasses.

'Shall I say when?' she asked.

Too pert she was. Too hoping he'd approve. Too eager, in her stateless way, to satisfy.

'I think I'd rather you didn't,' he said. 'One always has a tendency to know precisely when.'

He beckoned her a little nearer, and she found that when she came to him, when she came up close, and took the glass, and stood beside her

generous host, she could see the brownish rav-
agings, the many facial tarnishings, of a well-
bred man of means approaching fifty.

'Exquisite glasses,' she murmured. 'Are they
Irish?'

'Bohemian,' he said. 'They're from Bohemia,'
he clarified.

'Have you been there?'

'It's possible. Indeed it's fairly probable. But
please don't feel the need to entertain. Don't
exert yourself, excessively, in making conversation. This isn't what one used to term a
cocktail-party, and I frankly doubt you'd be
here, if it were.'

She swallowed what he'd given her, and
tasted aniseed. She never drank, if she could
help it, if she could possibly avoid it. Liquids of
an alcoholic nature always seemed to let her
down. They always seemed to loosen her. They
made her melt and flow.

'So I shouldn't speak at all,' she said. 'In case
it bothers you, I mean.'

His tongue flicked out and licked pale lips.

'It doesn't really bother me, tremendously.
But basically, you've got it right. Basically, I'd
like you not to verbalise.'

He frowned at the stripped-oak floor.

'That's what I'd like,' he said.

'Basically . . .' she prompted.

He nodded, for he knew she'd got his drift, she'd understood what he was saying. She seemed a fairly understanding kind of girl.

'It's nothing personal, as such,' he said. 'But I have a good idea of what you'd want to say, at any given moment. Your oral self-expression doesn't really interest me. I know, you see, before you start.'

The words kept coming, although his mouth was barely open. The sounds emerged, as if by magic, from the small and slit-shaped aperture, the pursed and prissy hole.

'There's something so depressing, so dreadfully predictable, in what might pass for thoughts inside your brain. I simply have to look at you, and I know what's in your head. I know you're standing there, quite stupidly, consumed and eaten up with fear – though doubtless in a moist and female way – and I find this knowledge that I have, this premonition of your state of mind, completely and profoundly boring.'

He gazed at her, and thought of what they'd do a little later. He pictured all the pleasures they might share. The fun they'd have, the pair of them. Or him, at least. The himness of the fun would be spectacular.

'And correct me if I'm wrong,' he said, 'but I think, essentially, you're here to relieve my boredom.'

He removed a pale blue handkerchief from a trouser pocket, and waved it at the floor. Might as well begin, he thought. Better get stuck in. No time like the present, if he recalled correctly, had always been his motto, the brief and pithy code by which he lived.

'If you wouldn't mind,' he murmured, 'stepping over here. Beneath the light, if I could bother you. If it's not too much to ask.'

He gave a small, self-conscious bow. A tiny act of genuflection.

'Forgive the imposition.'

She did as she was told, and stepped beneath the light. Being somewhat short of funds, lacking what is called a valid entry permit, and having grown, quite rapidly, quite fond of Little Venice, she did as she was told and stood beneath the light.

He looked her up and down, discovering a strange, obscure excitement in the cheapness of her clothes. The shell-pink, viscose blouse, the coal-black, calf-length skirt. The whole ensembled testament to the arts of mass-production.

He held her chin and tipped her face away from him, assessing shape and texture, noting with delight the slightly undernourished puffiness. The complexion showed, he felt, a rather pleasing lack of nutrients. She must have gorged on carbohydrate, indulged herself in too much worker-food.

'Not bad,' he said, 'not bad . . .'

He ran his fingers across her cheek and stroked the unfamiliar skin, then turned her head aside and examined the convoluted ear.

He squeezed the lobe, for no apparent reason, and watched her try to squirm away.

'Not exactly *good*, mind . . .'

He narrowed his eyes, for he had to be sure.

'But definitely not bad.'

Mine, he thought, triumphantly. All mine.

He poked a thumb between her lips, and prised them open. He thumbed her foreign lips apart, and peered inside.

'I'll fix your teeth for you,' he said. 'That's what I'll do, should we stay together, should we learn to coexist. Have them fixed one day, if you behave.'

He spat into the piece of cloth. He expectorated manfully, and a single strand, a spittle-thread which glistened in the light, remained dangling from the corner of his mouth.

'Sometimes females don't appreciate that cleanliness is something to be cherished.'

He took the piece of moistened cloth and wiped her bravely upturned face.

'They're not aware that germs are sadly prevalent, in those from overseas. Visitors who come here with their droplet-spread diseases.'

A shriek of laughter erupted from below. It came from half-way down the street, and bounced inside the room.

'If you've any questions, now's the time to spew them out. Now's the time to voice concerns. No point moaning later, once I'm in my stride.'

She pondered, for a moment. She contemplated thoughtfully, reflected on his kind and generous offer. It was nice of him to ask, at least. Big of him to make the effort. So better spew it out, she thought. Now's the time to voice concerns. No point moaning later, once he's in his stride.

'If I ever want you to stop . . .' she ventured.

'Just say the word.'

'And you'll stop.'

'I will.'

'You're sure of that?'

'I'm positive.'

'And if I can't speak . . .'

'I'm sorry?'

'My mouth,' she said. 'You might have . . .'

'Ah, yes. Of course. I might indeed. Well make a sign, some kind of movement. I'm always rather *good* on body language.'

'And if, for any reason, I'm not able to move . . . ?'

He clicked his teeth in irritation. He frankly couldn't bear it when they started being difficult.

'I'll know,' he said.

'But how?'

'Because I'll empathise. And when I empathise, I do so absolutely.

'So what you do will be with my consent?'

'Correct.'

He rearranged a cuff.

'Broadly with your consent.'

He allowed himself a wealthy sort of smirk.

'The things I do will be with your broad consent.'

'And you'll stop whenever I want.'

'Of course.'

'I only have to say the word.'

'Or make a sign.'

'And first you'll empathise.'

'Indeed.'

'And then you'll stop.'

'I shall.'

He scratched his chin.

'Most probably.'

He leaned across and removed her almost empty glass.

'Unless I have a particular desire, at that particular moment, to continue.'

'Then you won't stop . . .'

'No.'

He wiped the rim where her lips had been. He took a freshly laundered napkin, and wiped away her sediment.

'But I *will* empathise.'

3

A wave of overwhelming gratitude engulfed her.

She knew this day would be the turning-point, the first, delightful taste of darker pleasures, yet to come. Those words he used, the slight, ironic tone, that mocking voice, the way he wiped her glass. All touched her in a single, shining instant of perception, and in honour of the moment, there were stirrings down below. For viciousness quite often breeds lubriciousness.

'How often might it happen?'

'Not too often, I would have thought.'

He spread his lips. He let her see the clear and perfect brightness of his unselfconscious smile.

'Anticipation is the key.'

He put his hand against her back. The cleft and hollow of her back was where he pressed his hand.

'I think it's time to start,' he said. 'Time to have a go.'

He moved her on ahead.

'If you'd care to step outside . . .'

His pressure on her unresisting back.

'I'm sure it won't take long.'

He reached in front of her and pushed the door.

'One likes to be informal.' He eased her gently through. 'One aims at being fairly unpretentious.'

When she went inside the hall the air was cooler, almost chilly. There was the faintest reek of middle age. A tinge of rotting gut. A suggestion of decay. Not entirely all-pervading, but still a whiff was there. She walked along the corridor, and felt his hand slide further down, until it found itself a modest niche, a small, secluded place in which to ruminate.

'We'll try our best to improvise. Start with something simple, and take it on from there. There has to be a build-up, a gradual escalation.'

The ruminating fingers down below.

'Because in all things, especially these things, I think you'll find that there's a necessary escalation.'

The damp, delicious breath against her neck.

'So there's no point holding back,' he said, 'there's no point being shy.'

And she mentally agreed, she silently concurred, as he fingered what was precious, and they padded down the hall.

The bathroom, he assured her, was absolutely genuine. He led her in, and pointed to the floor and walls. All marble, he pronounced. From Italy, he added. There was nothing imitation, in his very favourite room.

She bent to touch the phone beside the toilet seat.

'Can I ring home, from time to time?'

'Of course you can. Reverse the charges, if you wish.'

He felt quite philanthropic.

'Let Mummy know how well you've done.'

It didn't take too long to fill the bath. Water powered from the taps. It gushed and thundered down. He ripped apart a sachet, and let the cream spurt out, and watched it start to foam.

'I've never been too keen on showers. Speaking for oneself,' he mused, 'one's always thought a bath is so much nicer.'

Rolling up his sleeves, he dipped an elbow in the water, checking it, in case the guest should prove too sensitive, estimating temperature, ensuring all was ready for his grimy lady-friend.

'Please get undressed,' he said. 'Disrobe, if you prefer.'

She stared at him – the briefest hesitation, a clouding of the eyes, a memory of spending time in Dagenham – then pulled apart the buttons of her blouse. (The pencil-skirt, of which he seemed quite fond, took slightly longer to remove.)

'About the money . . .' she suggested, as she carefully unzipped.

He gazed at her, and couldn't help but shudder at her lack of self-respect. He was a cultivated man, and he quivered, for a second. There was the barest tremor of surprise, the slightest grimace of distaste. He removed his elbow from the water, hoping that she wouldn't make a scene.

Of all the questions she could have raised, she had to raise the money-question. How typical, he thought, of those who lacked a scrotum. How vulgar they could often be. They somehow always had to spoil things, they always had to puncture the illusion. The damp, alluring, ever-twitching little bitches always had to whinge, and whine, and try to pick his pocket, before the game had even started.

'Didn't I tell you in the cab?'

He showed his teeth. A flash of brittle sympathy.

'How very thoughtless. How very naughty. How very sad I am to tell you that there won't be any payment. No stipend, as it were. No spendables, I mean.'

A self-absolving shrug. He thought he'd made it clear . . .

'Satisfaction – possibly. Remuneration – not.'

And he held his blue-veined, bony hand in front of him, as if to keep her venal self at bay.

'To give you money would demean you.'

He flicked some creamy water at the sulking, foreign face.

'So demean me,' she replied.

He pulled her down beside him, entwined his fingers in her hair, and made a mental note to see she got a decent cut.

'I will,' he said, 'believe me.'

And he gently pushed her head beneath the foam.

4

He found she settled in remarkably. Although quite disinclined to cook a meal, or make the bed, or wash his generous smalls, she pandered to his tastes in many other ways. It was all proceeding rather well. The escalation he'd envisaged had been smoothly set in motion, and he found that she responded most agreeably.

It took a week or two to break her in, to help her understand the type he was, to make her comprehend the kind of thing he craved. Almost every night he turned the screw a little tighter, he upped the stakes and went a little further. The uncomplaining refugee was escalated, on an almost nightly basis.

When he found she was a Capricorn, pre-destined to be tethered, his pleasure was enormous. He gushed and flowed with happiness, he oozed with delectation, went limp with quiet contentment. He blessed the day, in short, he'd brought her back with him.

But nothing, sadly, is forever.

A month went past before he recognised they'd reached the summit of the practical, the peak of what was feasible, the apex of the possible. Max came and saw and conquered what he wanted, but had no sense of self-disgust, no feeling of revulsion, no conscious-ness of doing something dirty. It was downhill all the way. Diminishing returns.

So with boredom gnawing at his groin, he took the final plunge. In a brief and coded call, he offered all he had. He told a man he vaguely knew to come, and see, and savour.

He'd chosen what she wore, that night. He'd bought it for her specially, an expensive velvet sheath he'd somehow guessed would suit her. He'd picked it out from all the others on the rack, then had it wrapped and hand-delivered. He felt he'd spent too much on her, cash he could have spent on something else. He'd pulled out several newly-minted notes, and fanned them out for all to see, although it gave him pain to do so. It hurt him, in his throbbing guts, to have to buy her what she didn't have already, and what she didn't have already was so completely infinite.

But then one had to, he supposed. One had to spend a pound or two, one had to dig into one's unearned pile, and be prepared to offer up a morsel to a tradesman, if one wished to live a life appropriate to Little Venice.

He told her what it cost him, the excessive price he paid, and she spread her ruby lips, and flashed her smegma-tinted teeth in satisfaction. She looked so self-assured, that night, so perfect, in her over-painted way, that he had no choice, he knew he had no other option, but to twist her head away from him, and bite the bluish skin beneath her neck.

'It's not a gift,' he reminded her. 'Not yours to keep, forever. Just a shred of high-class cloth I've lent you, for a while.'

He touched the purple mark his teeth had left. He liked to brand her, now and then. He liked to suck the Bratislavan skin, and nibble tender bits of her. Even at her best, she tasted slightly rancid. There was an undertone, if nothing more, of someone past her sell-by date. He'd have to season her, he told himself. Spread his favourite garlic butter on that not-yet-wrinkled skin. His mouth began to gurgle at the salivating prospect. He trickled at the thought of it, and ran an idle finger down the velvet-covered spine.

He had measured her himself. He'd wrapped

the tape across her breasts, and pulled it tight around her waist, and stretched it out around her hips, and slipped it, in his playful way, between her legs, then licked the toxic lead of the slim, lead-pointed pencil, and jotted down the measurements.

And he'd chosen well, he'd selected with an artist's eye. She would have had to say so, had he asked her. He could have gripped her by the arm and twisted something delicate, until she told him what he knew already, namely that he'd chosen rather well. He could have asked her, just to pass the time. He could have gently hurt her, could have made her quietly moan, at least to keep in practice. He could have done delicious things until she gave her usual sob, and finally admitted just how much it suited her, this dress he'd picked out from the rack, and watched them wrap, and made them hand-deliver.

He regarded her approvingly, despite himself. She wore it with panache, the money wasn't wasted. It clung to her like oil, that dress. It shone beneath the lamp, and seemed to make her glisten with excitement. He watched her make her oily way across the floor.

'You look quite good in black,' he said. 'It really rather suits you.'

'Every girl looks good in black.' She was generous to her sex, for once.

'Please don't contradict,' he said. 'Not tonight,' he added. 'Indeed not ever, but especially not tonight.'

'I was extending, not contradicting. Endorsing what you said, and applying it more generally.'

That struck him as a fairly decent mouthful, a surprisingly lucid lump of prose, for one so profoundly foreign. She must have learned it from the BBC. She must have lain in bed back home, dreaming of some green, more pleasant land, and pressed her scrubbed and straining ear to a plastic wireless in the dark.

'Black suits you,' he insisted. 'You should wear it more often.'

She spread her hands against her hips and slid them down the velvet sheath.

'Why does it suit me?'

Expectantly she asked him. She loved that dress, the feel of it, the way it clung to every hill and hidden valley.

His pink-rimmed eyes slid up and down. He wondered why it suited her. There must have been a reason why he'd said it.

'Because of what it hides,' he said. 'It conceals your lack of symmetry, your very many blemishes.'

She pouted, like a child. With quite emetic

winsomeness, she pushed her lower lip a fraction forward.

'Love me,' she demanded, 'love my blemishes.'

He sipped his drink and gazed at her. He felt triumphant, almost sated. He liked to keep her satisfied. Give her what she needed most. She asked for what she got, he thought. She bared her skin and begged for it.

'But I don't love you,' he pointed out.

With a few well-chosen words, in a single callous phrase, he pleasured her. He had this gift, this rare and giving gift, to say the things she longed to hear. Corrosive things she'd stroke, and lick, and nurture, because they meant he really cared.

So she smiled, as he'd expected. She dipped her head in gratitude, and stared at what he wore: the stiff, white shirt, the dinner-jacket, the cummerbund. The whole patrician style of it, the sight of him contained like that, held back and kept in check, enchanted her.

Perhaps she had an inkling of the glories yet to come, but even so, the self-restraint, the chivalry, the abstinence before the feast, the rigid self-control of a man like that, with tastes like those – all this made her Balkan senses tingle with excitement, minutely oscillate with glee.

For what were manners, in a passive man? What was decency, in one who had no other choice, one who had no chance, on earth, of reaching out and taking what he wanted?

But when a man like Max was tender, when charming, brutal Max decided, on a passing whim, to treat her softly, to touch her gently, as the better kind of brute will often do, it had a meaning, after all. (Or so she thought, being thoughtfully inclined.)

That noble Max would choose to keep himself in check, for once, that he'd forgo his natural rights, his clammy needs and baser inclinations, and perversely *not* lash out, for once, could only make her want him more. For she knew that he was merely marking time. Resting, for a while, before responding to the call of duty.

But the tiny verbal barbs, those little poison-drops that dripped, with such consuming ease, from such amusing lips, would do for now. They'd make the waiting so much less unpleasant. The best was yet to come, but this would do for now, this would keep her hanging on, these putrid sounds he made would keep her satisfied, for now.

She felt her brain begin to swell. She felt it start to pulse and throb. A thought occurred, and struggled for expression.

'Why mustn't I contradict you,' she enquired, 'tonight, in particular?'

He smiled at the foreign person. Being mellow with Scotch, and warm with anticipation, he would indulge her total insolence, her lack of comprehension. It came to him, quite suddenly, that there might be more of her, back home. In Budapest, or Bucharest, or wherever else she came from. There might be clones of her, there might be sweetly glowing doubles, perspiring imitations of his foundling. They'd turn up at his door one day, an endless, pallid line of them, a huge, malnourished regiment of stateless types with hungry eyes, all mutely waiting to be serviced, all quietly longing to be pleasured.

'You mustn't contradict,' he said, 'because we shan't be dining just *à deux* tonight. We have a guest, and I want you to behave. Treat him like a lesser form of me, a more prosaic version of your master. Be nice to him. Surpass yourself. Pretend that you're refined.'

He pulled back his cuff, and glanced at his watch.

'Sit with your legs crossed, and eat with your mouth closed.'

He couldn't help but smirk. He couldn't stop his mouth from smirking, should it so desire, for he loved to say that kind of thing. He loved to keep her on her toes, remind her that she

wasn't quite appropriate. (Though he'd over-
look it, for the present. He'd let it pass, for
now.)

'If he tries to touch you, you can let him.
Gropes are not allowed – not until we're on the
coffee – but casual touchings are permitted.
Touchings might be overlooked, though I doubt
he'll bother, while he's eating. The meal will
keep him occupied. They tend to like their food,
you know. That sort.'

'Which sort?'

'His affectations tend to grate. On me, I mean.
I don't suppose you'll even notice. He's quite
the expert, quite the little foodie. You'll be
competing with the Beijing duck, which means
that you'll probably lose. But if he does try, if he
does pause between courses, and wipes his
greasy lips, and casts a glance across the table,
and makes a tentative suggestion – to aid his
digestion – you have my permission to comply.'

He pushed her back against the wall, and
pressed her with his knee. He kneed her where
he knew she always needed it.

'He's the guest, my love, and we must cherish
our guests.'

His urgent face gazed down, the blue-black
stubble poking through. The whole entrancing
beauty of her sweetly bitter host.

She often liked to watch him shave. She'd sit

31

there on the toilet-seat, and watch him dip the razor in a sink of scummy water, and pull the sharpened blade across his skin. A week ago, as she was sipping cappuccino from his second-favourite cup, he'd smiled at her reflection, then missed his stroke and cut himself. A clean and inch-long cut, which split the skin above his lip. He touched a finger to his mouth, and smiled at her again, and hit her with the leather strop.

Although it seemed, to both of them, a very fair reaction, it made his second-favourite china cup describe a perfect arc, and smash down on the marble tiles. She imagined, for a second, that the shards and splinters formed a pattern. She watched him wipe away the red, and glance down at the floor, and try to analyse the pattern of his second-favourite cup, then look at her and lash her once again. But still she liked to watch him shave. Even when he used the strop, and even when he didn't, she liked to see him hold a blade. She liked to watch him scrape away the shadow.

But it was always there again, by dinner-time. Back the stubble always came, spreading like a charcoal stain across his pastel jaw. Every single night, he'd lead her to the table, pull out a high-backed dining chair, and ease it slowly forward. And as she sank down on the seat, he'd murmur something heartless in her ear, and she'd feel the bristled chin against her cheek, and think how glad she was, how truly fortunate, to have found a man like Max. And every single night, she allowed herself a tiny ooze of gratitude. For how could she have guessed, in the wilds of eastern Europe, that the earth contained such swarthy Anglo-Saxons?

And now there was a guest, as well. Another gentleman to teach her things. Another one to play with. A friend of Max to entertain.

'Is he my type?' she wondered.

'I never quite imagined you'd presume to have a *type*,' he said. 'He's not like me, should that be what you mean.'

'Not quite,' she said, but let it pass.

'He's modestly attractive, in a vulgar sort of way. If you like them dark and gipsy, he's your man.'

'But I'm not sure I'm too partial to vulgarity . . .'

(As if she were the choosy kind, who'd sift and trawl and pick the best, and wouldn't go with anyone who'd feed, and fuck, and fondle her.)

'You might well find him rather male. Quite a lad, in point of fact. Has no pedigree, of course. Lacks what one would class as class. An upstart, so to speak, of Semitic derivation. But women seem to like him, though I've heard he's rather picky where he sticks his pricky.'

33

He beamed at her.

'Is that your type?'

She sipped her brandy. Knowing that she didn't like the taste of alcohol, he often made her drink a glass or two. He'd pinch her nose and pour the liquid down her throat. He claimed it was his modest contribution to building up her character. He said he had to educate her palate, teach her to enjoy the better things in life. You'll acquire a taste for it, he told her, if you only persevere. Just let me force you, to begin with, and eventually you won't object. And when you're hooked, you'll want it all the time.

'Your friend,' she said, 'the dinner-guest. He's here because of business?'

Max shook his head.

'Because of pleasure.'

His pale and mirthless eyes.

'He's here because of you.'

He held the pear-shaped bottle by the hips.

'I've told him all about you.'

He filled her half-full glass.

'He wants to play the game.'

5

Of all the moments that she'd had, this was surely one to relish. For here she was, a no-body, a scrap of pungent nothingness, washed up in Little Venice. And so adored, so vital to his self-esteem, so central in his life. Abandoned on the street, and God had found her Max. A providential hand had brought her to his door, then held her down so she could kneel, and kiss, and worship. She savoured this most sweet of moments. She let it linger on her tongue.

What a pleasant way to live. What a lucky little bitch.

'I do hope he's polite,' she said. 'I do like men who like to be polite.'

Max waved a hand dismissively. (She had her points, he mused. Her moist and simple virtues.

It could have been quite beastly, if she hadn't been a sport.)

'Of course he is, when he really tries. And frankly, he's been trying all his life.'

'Have you always felt so hostile to your friends?'

He stared at her, admiringly. She was learning to provoke.

'If you mean our dinner-guest,' he said, 'that waiting slab of plebby expectation, I'm afraid you've misconstrued.'

He took her empty glass and placed it on the mantelpiece. He'd try to put it simply, to help her understand.

'I have colleagues, and acquaintances, and types with whom I copulate. I seem to have few friends, and those I have, I do indeed detest. But he isn't one of those, my love. Not exactly, no. Not quite the type I'd care to call a friend.'

'What would you call him?'

'A non-friend, I'd have thought, if you want to be precise. If you really want to pin me down.'

'Have you known him long?'

'Tangentially, for years.'

'You don't know him very well.'

'As I said, he's not a friend. He's not someone I'd confide in. I wouldn't trust him with my money.'

'But you're prepared to trust him with me.'

He smiled at her. How quick she was, when the need arose.

'Will I warm to him?'

'I somehow doubt it. One might even term your liking him perverse, if one recognised the word had any meaning. So warming won't occur. Combustion might prove difficult. If I've judged correctly, and I think I have, he'll arouse in you what might be termed an imprecise distaste.'

'No more than that?'

'It seemed enough, to start with. Disgust, of course, comes later. Consider it a learning experience. Consider him my guest. Consider yourself privileged. Consider the matter closed.'

He took her hand in his.

'Shall we go through?'

He led her down the corridor, and through an archway, and into what he liked to call the library. The silent man who waited there, the dinner-guest, was standing by the unlit fire. He wore a handmade suit of midnight blue, and as she gazed at him it came to her, quite suddenly, that imprecise distaste was not her most immediate reaction.

'This is Bruno,' Max pronounced. 'Bruno, this is her.'

He held the foreign arm. He gripped it quite excessively.

'My dear and good friend, Bruno. He's been wanting to meet you for weeks. Dying to meet you for days. Aching to meet you all evening. So say hello, why don't you.'

She felt herself begin to warm. She felt the lubrication flow.

'I gather you're the new boy.'

So young, he seemed. So completely flawless.

'I do hope you'll fit in.'

The new boy took her hand and brushed it with his lips. (How chivalrous, he was. How almost Continental.) He glanced across at Max.

'As ever, you were right,' he said. 'A minute in her company, and I already feel provoked. Well done, old son.'

The older man inclined his head to accept the praise.

'I'd never lie to my dearest friend. I'd fib, perhaps, but never lie. I'd never bring you here for nothing.'

The flushed and waiting object of their indiscreet desire turned to face the host. She had that look she always wore when needing explication.

'Does he mean provoked,' she asked, 'as in excited?'

(Her total love of self. Her glorious conceit.)

'No,' Max said. 'He's got a problem with the female of the species. I'm afraid I forgot to mention it. It must have slipped my mind. His woman-problem often gets him down, so I think he means provoked, as in provoked. Antagonised, is what he means.

'He means you're getting on his nerves, which is hardly too surprising, except he hasn't known you very long. He means there's too much traffic on the roads, and deals are getting harder, money's getting scarcer, time is getting shorter and he'd be really rather grateful, though he doesn't want to ask, if he could hit you.'

Max scratched a non-existent itch that came and went above his ear.

'I think you'll find that's what he means, when he says he feels provoked. That's more or less the gist. The subtext, as it were.'

Her naked shoulder felt the pressure of his hand. She felt him draw her slowly back, as if he feared that otherwise the dinner-guest might act too prematurely.

'But supper first.'

Her naked skin. The pressure of his hand.

'I'm sure we'll get to know each other, later.'

6

They stepped inside the pitch-black room. They stood near each other, close enough to feel the heat, but without quite touching. She could hear them breathing just behind her. Max's slight, asthmatic wheeze, and Bruno's unpolluted lungs. Her own reluctant breaths, her modest inhalations, barely made a sound. She wondered which of them would break the ice, and then, as if on cue, she felt a knuckled fist between her legs, and tried to ascertain, by what it tried to do, to whom it might belong.

'Can I hit her, now?'

Bruno's voice, thick with roasted meat and smooth with cognac. Such a strong young man. Such an appetite. But the lack of ambiguity, the soul-destroying bluntness, were vaguely disappointing. So literal a man, so lacking in finesse, might prove to be unsuitable. She might have moistened even sooner, had he been a shade more subtle – perhaps a wary circling round, the odd elliptical remark, the barest hint of doubt. But he was young, and the young were ever thus. At least he had some energy.

Max quietly cleared his throat and threw a switch. Three floor lamps flickered on, illuminating wood and brass and leather. A ceiling spotlight shafted down. They watched her flinch beneath the light. She looked disturbingly defenceless, standing in a threadbare slip, edged with artificial lace. They'd taken off her dress a while ago. Pulled it high above her head, and folded it, and placed it in the corridor. Now she stood and flinched and shivered, in the under-heated room.

'Can I hit her?' Bruno, once again. This time with the slightest touch, the merest hint, of petulance.

'No,' Max said. The rueful shrug, for he prided himself, amongst many things, on his seamless hospitality. It seemed so base, so churlishly ungenerous, to refuse.

'Might I ask why not?' Bruno didn't want to stir things up, but he felt he ought to know.

'She wouldn't like it,' Max explained. (The feebleness of his response. Its utter lack of relevance.)

Bruno peered at what he wanted, and recognised a sudden need to bruise her.

'But *I* might like it,' Bruno said. 'And I'm the guest.'

Max turned to her.

'And he's the guest.'

The newboy touched her foreign skin.

'She has to learn to integrate.'

He kneaded the soft and stateless flesh.

'She's got to learn our little ways.'

He sucked his teeth, and gently squeezed. He did his best to make her cry.

'Learn to mix and mingle.'

Max couldn't bear to let him down.

'Perhaps a little later, then.' He felt so altruistic. The guest would have his chosen entertainment.

'When we've finished off the port, and we're sitting feeling mellow, we might, perhaps, decide to beat her.'

Max dug his greedy fingers in between her folds.

'Though not too hard, one hopes?'

'Just pinching, slapping. Things like that.' Bruno, quick to reassure. 'Nothing heavy. Nice and friendly.'

And he pinched her, in a friendly kind of way.

'I prefer the slip left on,' he added. 'If it's all the same to you . . .'

(The demands they make, she thought. The ritual and the fantasy. And all to boost the flabbiness of their flabby, phallic desire.)

'As you wish,' Max said. 'It's only nylon, I'm afraid, but it's all she had. At first I thought I'd wrap her up in silk, something rather chic to match the dress, but nylon's somehow more authentic.'

Bruno raised a brow, regarded her anew.

'I take your point. She's got that kind of *nylon* aspect.'

'She has. One looks at her and thinks of rationing, and bread queues, and social deprivation. Lives of bovine drudgery, and bouts of civil strife.'

'I suppose she must be poor, then?'

'Desperately, old chum.' Max sighed with great contentment. 'So poor, in fact, it's almost sordid.'

And they stared at her, this nylon type, this bewitching bit of nothing, who exuded such delightful squalor. She seemed enchantingly beyond the pale. She seemed so far beneath them, so caked in some exotic dung, that they could have gone down on their knees and worshipped her, they could have pushed their eager faces up against her holy place, and worshipped at her temple. The very thought of being sullied only made them want her more, increased their pure and dog-like urge to sniff, and lick, and slobber.

'You give her silk, and you'll only spoil her. You want to give her what she's used to: liver-wurst and Polish bread, that's all she really needs. Don't raise her expectations, and she won't be disappointed.'

'That's a fairly profound remark to make.'

'Kind of you to say so.'

'And it's really rather big of you to spare the time.'

'That's what are friends for.'

With which engaging *aperçu*, the newboy slid a hopeful hand inside her panties. Max watched the fingers ruminate beneath the cotton, then make their crab-like way across the stretch of open ground he knew so well. What once was his alone, would now be shared. He managed not to shudder, but only just.

'This might sound strange,' he said, 'but I'd be grateful if you didn't. Not just yet. Not straight away. Not grope, I mean.'

He fumbled for the words.

'If you could wait a while, until I'm ready, I'd be obliged.'

'I'm not groping' – Bruno, quite aggrieved – 'I'm only fondling. She doesn't mind. I know

44

she doesn't, because if she did I'm sure she'd say so.'

'Fair point,' Max said. 'She's never been slow to open her mouth. Not orally reluctant, as it were. But if you wouldn't mind refraining, for a minute. Bear with me while I sort things out.'

He waved an arm towards the leather couch, the plushly padded chairs, the embroidered velvet cushions strewn across the carpet. (Not to mention all the implements, of different shapes and thicknesses, hanging on the walls. Mustn't mention those.)

'This is what we call the romper-room,' Max said. He pecked her lightly on the cheek, and held her firmly by the breast. 'It's where we like to romp.'

Both the boys had eaten well, almost to excess. They'd shown a lack of self-restraint, in matters calorific. She, however, had picked and nibbled at her meal, conscious of what lay ahead. The thought of eating food and quaffing wine, beforehand, made her queasy. The very thought of being bloated, in the romper-room, was enough to make her vomit up the piece of masticated duck that lay inside her belly.

She was never one to stuff herself, before a session, although she tried to keep it quiet from Max. It wasn't the kind of failing that she'd care to have him know. Not the type of thing to tell him, if one could possibly avoid it. He'd only make her eat until replete, then make her eat some more, then finish off with after-dinner mints, and fetch a pair of velvet cushions and hold her, bent and retching, while he worked out how he'd do the business. One day she might inform him, but not just yet, she thought, as he led her, in her stockinged feet, across the Persian carpet. She sometimes wondered why she did it. And she sometimes wondered why she wondered.

He stood her by the creased and faded cushions, a piled-up heap of plum and damson, caught beneath the spotlight. If she were only patient, if she could just control herself, the boys would lay her down. If she could just forbear from being too demanding, allow them just a moment to prepare, they'd spread her out, and keep her still, and hold her firmly down. The salivating thought of being held, and spread, and happy. She felt controlled, contained, immensely grateful.

'Would you like her on the floor or on the sofa?' Max, the deferential host.

Bruno shrugged, the non-committal guest. 'As you wish,' he replied.

'No please,' Max insisted.

'The floor then,' Bruno said. 'And then,

perhaps, the sideboard. And later, if she's good, the sofa.'

Max found his guest's decisiveness quite comforting. He seemed a very manly kind of man. Not for him to agonise, not for him to ingratiate, to let her chip away until the piece of him that gave him courage, the single piece which made him what he was, the only piece that really mattered, was hanging limp between his legs.

'I think you might be rather good at this,' Max said. 'I can't be sure, but I think you might.'

He placed a hand on the bony shoulder, and slowly pushed her down. So light she was, the refugee, that a single hand of a single man was enough to push her down.

'Oh by the way,' he said, 'before we start, before we get revved up, feel free to have a drink.'

'I'm fine thanks,' Bruno said, although he knew he could have downed a dram or two, he could have polished off a tumblerful of Scotch.

'It's up there if you want it.'

'I'll pass, for now.'

'I thought you might be feeling fragile.'

'Is that a fact?'

'Afraid it is.'

'Not at all,' the newboy said. 'I'm raring to go.'

He bared his teeth and flexed his legs. Testosterone personified.

'Are you really?'

'Really what?'

'Raring.'

'Asbolutely.'

'That's good,' Max said. 'I'm glad you're raring, because if you weren't entirely raring, I might be worried. I'm glad you're so gung-ho, for it means I made the perfect choice,' he gripped her by the slender neck, 'and that makes me rather glad.'

The newboy pulled her panties off, which pleasured him, enormously. He slipped a pair of cushions beneath the pelvic bone, so that her hips rose up to greet him. Such brazen hips, such wanton globes. He jammed another cushion underneath.

'Do you think she's glad?' he asked, and realised, with a lurching shock of self-disgust, that he genuinely wanted to know.

'Not quite,' Max said. 'Anticipatory, perhaps. Most probably lubricous. But glad, I have my doubts. Glad is not the word that springs most readily to mind.'

He pushed her head away from him, tilting it so that the guest could see her profile.

'And examine, if you will, this face, and see the fear.'

'She's surely not afraid . . .' Bruno queried, ever hopeful.

'I would say so, yes. I'd say she's got a sense of creeping dread, to be precise, and precision often helps. For although she's kneeling down between us, quietly waiting with her usual damp decorum, although she's spread wide open, splayed and ready, with her save-me eyes and her hit-me smile, she's shaking within, she's quaking within, she's screaming inside, as well she might.'

On hearing which, the dinner-guest was seized by urges that he'd rarely had before, sophisticated needs which made him blush and coyly dribble.

He gripped her by the hips and pulled them even higher, so that the moist and waiting rump was jutting in the air, and her back was forced to dip, and the nylon slip rode up, and she muttered something meaningless in her Balkan mother-tongue.

7

'How do we do this, actually?'

'We do *her*, actually. It's share and share alike, *chez moi*. We share her, and she likes us. All for one, and one for all, you know the sort of thing. Brotherhood, and comradeship, and doing beastly things to little bitches.'

They squatted down on either side (at either end, to be exact), conscious of the mutely waiting form that might, they hoped, be quietly oozing in their honour. She looked so perfect, as she lay there. So disgustingly content.

Bruno gazed at what she had, and allowed himself to sigh, and almost bent to kiss the pinkly-glowing cheeks. He almost wrapped his eager lips around the secret opening. He almost probed it with his long, elastic tongue.

But he knew he'd never do it. He knew it

wasn't really *him*. For like many of his faith, like many of a kosher inclination, he kept an eye on what went in his mouth, he controlled his oral intake rather carefully. So perhaps he'd better not indulge, perhaps he'd better leave all that to Max. And he banished, with an effort, the self-abasing image. (Some things, he often thought, were better left to others.)

'Could we possibly blindfold her?' How green he was, how tentative. 'Because I'm not too keen on being watched.'

'Whatever you prefer.' Max swelled with generosity. He almost overflowed with magnanimity.

'But she won't be able to see you, as it happens. You won't be in her line of sight.'

'How so?'

'You'll be bringing up the rear, old son. A special treat' – he grinned his Maxie grin – 'if that's all right with you . . . ?'

The newboy stared at him with ancient, tribal eyes.

'Of course,' he said. 'No sweat.'

(Adapt or die, he told himself.)

'I've always thought the rear way is the best way,' Max explained, in case a rationale was needed. 'The good old tradesman's entrance: round the back, and in one goes. Rather like splitting a summer peach, if you take my point.'

'I believe I do.'

'Like sliding your knife right into the peach.'

'Right into the cleft.'

'The cleft of the peach.'

'The knife in the cleft.'

'And the juice starts to flow down the blade of the knife . . .'

'. . . in the cleft of the peach . . .'

'. . . and runs down the hilt, and over your fingers.'

Max squeezed her where she liked it least.

'If I'm not being too metaphorical . . .'

'Not at all,' Bruno assured him. 'Far from it, in fact.'

She was so completely theirs, that night, so peachified, so ready to be clefted. A luscious piece of forbidden fruit from some poor, benighted land. They would tunnel their way inside, that night, they would delve so deep inside, they'd plough so sure a furrow, that even should they pass away, some corner of her foreign field would be for ever England.

'But I want to tell you something. Shall I tell you?'

'Please.'

Max paused and frowned. He'd give the Bruno-boy his insights, the wisdom gleaned from years of observation. He lowered his voice. (Whisper it not.)

'I don't like it, when they like it from the rear. If you follow,' he confided. 'If you get my drift.'

'I think I do,' the guest replied, 'but just in case I don't, perhaps you could explain. If you'd care to clarify, I'm sure I'd be obliged.'

'Simply put, there's something wrong with girlies when they like it from behind.'

'Does she . . .' Bruno ventured, '. . . would you say she's partial?'

'Afraid she is, old mate.' Max pulled his lower lip, perturbed and deep in thought. 'Very partial, blast her.'

He shrugged and sighed and rearranged her head. Perhaps she couldn't help it. It took all sorts, these days. He wasn't one to judge, nor would he be the first to cast a stone.

He was good to her, he told himself. Too good, perhaps. Too often too obliging. But he couldn't help but empathise, he couldn't help but comprehend what she was feeling, at that moment. For he sensed the tremors, and felt the quivers, and knew within his bones what bliss it was, for an emigrée, to be spread upon those cushions.

Well, must press on, he told himself. Give her what she's waiting for, before she starts to sulk.

'Shall I lead, or shall you?'

'You're the host.'

'Aren't I just?'

The smirk was almost audible. Max moved his weight a little to the left, opened the whalebone buttons of his flies, moved her shoulders fractionally to the right, wound his fingers through her tinted hair, smiled with damp collusion at his guest and said (for he was an educated man, who relished the chance of a decent chinwag):

'Things are fairly grim, you know, across the Channel.'

Bruno raised a doubtful eyebrow. 'Is that a fact?'

'I would have thought so,' Max continued, and jerked up her head with what might have seemed, to the casual observer, an excess of zeal. He placed a dry, patrician hand between his thighs.

'With the Left discredited . . .'

He pulled out his stiff and sweating pride.

'. . . and thuggery somewhat rampant . . .'

Emitting a well-bred grunt, he heaved himself inside her mouth.

'. . . things are looking rather bleak. One doesn't want to dwell on it, but the walls do seem to be closing in.'

'On foreigners.'

'Sorry?'

'Those walls you mentioned.'

Bruno, squatting close behind her, thought it time to have his say.

'It's surely not *our* kind they're closing in on. It's only foreign sorts. Types like that. One aches for them, of course . . .'

'Of course.'

'. . . but life goes on.'

'It does.'

'I suppose we're lucky no one knows she's here.'

'Incredibly lucky.'

'We might have had to hand her in.'

'Or make a noble gesture and hide her.'

'Or even hand her in.'

'We might have had to.'

'Yes.'

Max held her head and pressed it firmly down into his groin. He looked reflective, deep in thought, in a princely kind of way. Intent on both his musing and his oozing.

'She speaks the language well enough.'

'And she looks the part.'

'She does,' Max said. 'Could almost be a native.'

'But she's not quite one of us though, is she.'

The newboy staked his claim to be included in the in-group.

'Isn't she?'

'Not quite, no,' the almost Anglo-Saxon guest concluded.

'But she's not entirely one of them.'

55

'She's neither us nor them.'

(The nuances, the manifold gradations.)

'She's an in-betweener.'

'That's why we want her,' Max suggested.

'*Do* we want her?'

'I think we do.'

Max felt her twitch, he felt her give a tiny, shameless shudder. He ground the hidden face into his groin.

'Do you mind if I press on?'

'Please do. You do your stuff, you forge ahead, and I'll catch up later.'

'If you're quite, quite sure . . .'

'Oh absolutely.' Bruno, taking pains to be a gentleman. 'There's no point waiting, as you're ready.'

How true, Max thought, how very true. He glanced, with mild amusement, at what lay, with fake reluctance, in his lap. It suited her like that, he thought, it suited her to be so docile. He noticed that he'd slightly moved his hands. He'd moved them off her cranium, and slid them past her temples, until they held the handles on the sides. That's interesting, he thought, and shared the revelation with his guest.

'They're handy, aren't they?'

'Women?' Bruno prompted, trying not to sound too adolescent.

Not without affection, Max was gazing at her bobbing head. He gripped the lobes a little harder.

'Their ears,' he said, and shut his eyes and let her have her way with him.

Minutes ticked away, whole sixty-second chunks of self-indulgence. Minutes of what passed for bliss in the upper reaches of Little Venice. He held her down and let the goodness flow.

'I think she's choking.'

Bruno's urgent whisper pierced the air. The wide-eyed newboy, backing off already. How typical, Max thought, how totally suburban. Trust the little turd to try and spoil it.

'She's not,' Max said, 'believe me.'

'You're sure of that?'

'One's fairly sure.'

A smothered gurgle came from down below.

'Not absolutely *positive*, but then one never is, these days. But honestly, I wouldn't worry. She twitches, on occasion. She gets these spasms, now and then.'

'How often does she get them?'

Max frowned in concentration. Now there's a thought, he thought.

'Not too often. Spasmodically, in fact. That's why we tend to call them spasms.'

The newboy nodded doubtfully, but didn't

57

like to interfere, in case the host took umbrage. He merely watched her buck and heave, and listened to the noise.

'I suppose it might be a choking-spasm . . . ?'

'Might be,' Max concurred. 'Or it might be just a pleasure-spasm. I dare say she could tell us which, but I'd rather not enquire just now. Let's leave her, for the moment.'

He looked apologetic.

'One shouldn't interrupt when they're chewing on the cud.'

Which sounded fair enough, the houseguest thought. Civilities should be observed. Standards ought to be maintained, when all was said and done. He watched her shake with might-be pleasure-spasms.

'By the way,' he said, 'before I get stuck in,' he added, 'thought I'd better let you know I'm on a double yellow. Didn't want to bother you, but thought I'd better mention it.'

Bruno eased himself a little closer in behind her. Nearer to the action. The demurely waiting plumpness of the rumpness.

(She felt the warmth of him, the glowing heat, an inch or two away. That's what she felt, should her feelings be of interest.)

'So I hope I won't be ticketed, is all I wish to add.'

He pulled the metal zip the whole way down.

She trickled quietly when she heard the noise it made, a thin and slightly vulgar sound. (The zip, that is, and not the trickle.)

'I'm afraid it's rather possible you might be clamped,' Max said. 'I suppose I should have warned you.'

'So you should, old son. Indeed you should. I'll be profoundly mortified to find my motor towed away.'

He pushed his knees between her legs.

'It's not the money,' he added quickly, 'it's the dreadful inconvenience.'

'And then there's the money.'

'Precisely.'

Now it was Bruno's turn to realign, and re-adjust, and get the angle right. He slid his hands beneath her thighs and eased them open. Anxious to explore, and being of a pioneering nature, he tried to peer inside, but the sweetly-smelling passage remained intriguingly obscure.

'Shall I do my stuff, then?' Bruno queried. 'What with *tempus fugit*, and the parking situation?'

'Fire away, old fruit.'

When Max leaned forward it made her gag, if not regurgitate, as the best of him, his core and essence, lightly brushed against her tonsils. She felt his fingers sliding down her dipped and aching back and come to rest a little further on.

She somehow knew that Bruno tensed behind her. She somehow knew he braced himself, he almost took the plunge, and she somehow knew he glanced at Max.

'If it's all the same to you,' he murmured. 'If you really wouldn't mind . . . ?'

The exchange of knightly courtesies, permission sought and gladly granted.

'Be my guest,' Max said, urbanely gracious to a fault, and spread her cheeks apart, as a good host always should.

8

Now that they'd become acquainted, now they'd shared a meal of Beijing duck and watched each other masticate, it seemed to be appropriate that Bruno took up residence. He was young, and fit, and willing to oblige. And he more than paid his way, which often helps in tenancy arrangements.

'I'll take the blue room, shall I?'

(The self-sustaining confidence, the breeziness of Brunos, when they think they've found a home.)

'Always been quite fond of blue. Quite partial, so to speak.'

'It's hyacinth.'

'Tremendous news.'

The newboy's things, such as they were – his artefacts and trunk of clothes – were ferried to the house, and carried up the five stone steps, and laid out in the chosen room. A splendid sight, they made: himself spread out in perfect heaps.

'I'll unpack later, if I may.'

'Feel free,' Max said.

'I'll do my best.'

By the time they ate their supper in the library – some kind of stew, with farmhouse bread – she'd gone upstairs, and got undressed, and slipped between the sheets. (She'd claimed she had a headache, and who were they to disagree.) Max had made her swallow phenobarbitone, and waited while she fell asleep, and now he watched the newboy wiping breadcrumbs from his mouth.

'You seemed to cope quite well,' Max said, 'for one so unprepared. A little clumsy, possibly, but I'm sure she didn't mind.'

'Does she always sob like that?'

'Now and then,' Max said. 'She sometimes cries, but I don't know why.'

'I hope it wasn't me.'

'I rather think it was. You weren't entirely tender.'

'No?'

'A slight excess of relish, frankly.'

'I've always been what's known as keen.'

'Commendable, of course, but we really have to synchronise.'

'I take your point.'

'I thought you might.'

Autumn rain was hissing on the pavement, their preciousness was fast asleep upstairs, and the pair of them were sitting at the table, smoking cigarillos and digesting what they'd eaten.

Bruno felt the evening's gases gather in his belly. They pressed against his lower gut and clamoured for release. Should he bring them up, or send them down? Release them from the mouth, or from the rear? An interesting conundrum, which reminded him of her.

'She's quite a noisy little thing.'

'But she has her pride.'

'Indeed she does. When one thinks of her, one often thinks how proud she is.'

'Not to mention dignified.'

'I'm sure she's basically a lady.'

'Deep down inside.'

'A dame with depth.'

'An arse with class.'

'A vulgar image . . .'

'But apposite, I would have thought.'

They spread their legs, and slowly smiled, and began to bond. Bruno leaned back in the chair and glanced around the room. There were shelves and shelves of books. Piles and heaps and wordy growths. A very bookish man, his host, a man who'd slide himself between the pages of his favourite piece of prose, and gently rub himself to sleep. Achieve a little friction with some fiction.

'I do like talking about her,' he mused.

'So do I,' the host agreed.

'In fact it's almost as satisfying *talking* about her as doing her.'

'Less aggravating, somehow.'

'She can be awfully difficult.'

'Dreadfully tiresome.'

'Such a surly girly.'

Max moved his stew-encrusted fork, smearing gravy round his plate. He'd cooked the meal himself, prepared it from a battered can and served it up for Bruno's delectation. The foulness of the food, he thought. The sheer inedibility. It served the newboy right.

'You've only got the one, I take it?'

Bruno pointed at a square of book-free wall. He aimed his Bruno-finger at the shotgun on the wall. It thrilled him, quite enormously. It made him throb and glow to be so close to what was lethal.

'The barrel's been cut down,' he said, as if Max hadn't noticed.

'Sawn off, to be exact. And double barrels, if one's counting, if one wants to be pedantic.'

'Is it legal, doing that?'

'I doubt it, but one gets these whims.'

'Short and stubby . . .'

'That's the style.'

Bruno sucked a piece of kidney from between his upper teeth. He'd never been too keen on stew, but didn't like to mention it. He felt it wasn't quite his place to pass opinions on the food.

'So there's just the one,' he said. 'You don't collect.'

'I've always found that one's enough. A single pair of sawn-off tubes has always been sufficient.'

'I suppose you've never used it . . .'

'Not as yet. But one keeps it loaded, just in case. One likes to keep it primed and ready.'

'In case of what?'

'Riff-raff breaking down the door, perverts climbing through the windows, defecating hooligans, girlies being surly . . .'

Bruno couldn't help but be impressed. Although endowed with liberal views, and being humanistically disposed, he found the sight of weaponry enchanting. He recognised the beauty of a smooth and polished barrel.

'Is it safe to handle?'

The urgent eagerness of newboys.

'I hesitate to put you off, but it's a fully-loaded shotgun.'

'So one shouldn't really play with it . . .'

'Better not,' Max said. 'Better play with something else.'

The conversation, they discovered, had put them in the mood. Their mutual love of metal, their interest in ballistics, reminded them of what was soft and helpless.

They woke her after midnight, although they'd promised not to. They'd given her their solemn word, they'd promised she could drift off into sleep, they'd said that no one would disturb her, and she'd let herself imagine she believed them. Their constant lies, their lovable deceits, seemed somehow only natural. It was part of their appeal, that they always let her down.

So when she heard the knuckles start to rap against her door, when she heard them softly knock inside her dream, her baser instincts made her jerk awake. The bits of her that seeped and gurgled sprang to life, and forced her sleeping brain to consciousness.

It took a while to remember where she was, which seemed to happen more and more, of late. She'd wake up in the dark and imagine, for a single, fragile instant, that she'd never gone away at all, she'd never left her unforgiving home, and was back where she belonged. But then she'd stretch and yawn and breathe the overheated air of the tiny space they'd granted her, and know that she was really here. It wasn't just a fantasy. She'd really found herself a piece of stucco-fronted paradise.

She looked across the room. The yellow light that pushed in from the hall was strong enough to silhouette their shapes inside the doorway. She saw them standing in their handmade suits, all stiffness kept concealed and out of sight. She recognised they'd dressed like this for her, in honour of whatever was to come. They'd wrapped themselves in cultivated style to let her know they cared, to show how much they valued her. (The combination being one that ladies often like: well-cut cloth, and no doubt rampant maleness; the vaguely thuggish beauty of the gentleman.)

She would have termed the way she felt, at that precise and flawless moment, a kind of nauseated readiness, had her fluency in English progressed that far. When she saw them standing in the doorway, hands plunged deep in trouser pockets, studiedly unhurried and completely unconcerned, a brutal silence keeping their brutality in check, she could have spewed with glee, she could have vomited with joy, she could have retched in stateless ecstasy. They'd come for her. The boys were here. Her hard and luscious boys.

They were silent, quite immobile, black against the light. She waited quietly for a voice, some oral indication of the role she'd have to play. She wanted them to speak to her, to tell her what she had to do, for like many of the rootless sort, she had a desperate and abiding need for certainty.

'She looks quite . . .'

'Doesn't she.'

'So unprepared . . .'

'Endearingly.'

She loved it when they talked like that, when they started their seduction with these tender verbal spurts.

'I suppose we must have woken her.'

'She shouldn't sleep.'

'Why ever not?'

'It's bad for her.'

That tone of voice, that Maxiness. She dribbled with delight.

'Do you think she'd like it if we . . . ?'

'Possibly.'

'Perhaps we ought to ask . . .'

'And perhaps we'd better not. One wouldn't care to set a precedent.'

'But I must admit,' the newboy said, 'I sometimes wonder what it is she really wants.'

The slightly taller shape, the one she recognised as Max, stepped inside the room, and wafting close behind there came an aftershave of rare and precious quality, for Max was such a sweetly scented man, so perfumed, in his scrotal way. Not a man to sweat, or have excessive odours. Not a very smelly man at all.

'She wants to die,' he said. 'She's aching for it. Waiting to be put to sleep. Dreaming of the day we finish her, completely.'

He came towards the bed. There was a blurred and rapid movement of his hands, and then a click, a small, blue flame, and suddenly, a reddish-orange glow. She could hear him breathing in, inhaling with a faint, congested wheeze, as he sucked the filtered smoke inside his lungs. Those lungs must be a sight, she thought, a vision of putrescence. Perhaps there was a little pool of tar within his chest, a black and stagnant pond in which he'd one day dip her face. It appealed to her, this side of him, this slightly rancid side.

The newboy quietly coughed. He often coughed, when Max lit up. He even smoked, occasionally, although one couldn't tell by watching him. Giving him a cool, appraising look, drinking in the physical perfection, one hardly would believe the newboy was a smoker.

Max came around the bed. Sucking more

serenely on his filter cigarette, he stepped around the side of the displaced person's bed. The mattress shifted slightly, when he leaned his weight against it. He nudged it with his thigh, and made it move beneath her. She felt the shudder of the bed, and her skin began to crawl, her flesh began to tighten with foreboding. Anxieties engulfed her. Trepidations, and other nice sensations.

He stood so close, pressed right against the bed, pressed hard against the pale bleached wood of her displaced person's bed. The muted rustling of a Max, as he prepared himself. The noble Bruno profile in the doorway. The self-effacing menace of her very favourite hosts.

It could have been too much for her, she almost might have given in, declared her nerve-ends couldn't take it, but she didn't. Even so, their nearness made her tremble, their closeness stripped away her self-control. Her weaker parts began to quiver, and she felt the fear come trickling out.

Max cleared his throat. (Sputum was his middle name.)

'We're trying something new today. Being more adventurous. Pushing back the boundaries of science.'

He moved a hand towards his mouth, cupped the cigarette inside his palm, took another drag, and then the red and burning tip came arcing down towards her face. Balletically, he brought it down. He held the glowing butt above her cheek, close enough for her to feel the heat, to understand what he might do to her, what he might just give way and do, were he so inclined.

She watched his fingers hold the stub above her face, quite near her nose, and not too far beneath her eye. Not me, she thought. Not that, she thought, then saw him jerk the cigarette away, and let it drop, and heard him grind it on the polished floor.

He cleared his throat again.

'We thought we'd spend some special time with you.'

She imagined she could almost hear him smiling. She was glad she'd made him smile. She was glad she'd given him some brief and fleeting pleasure, enough to make him spread his lips and almost smile. He touched her chin, and turned her face towards him.

'Some quality time.'

He bent a little closer. Whisky on his breath.

'Bruno's told me he's becoming rather bored . . .'

He placed a finger on her mouth.

'. . . and I'm afraid one can't endure, one simply can't abide, a bored and whining Bruno.'

He pushed the rigid finger past her lips and in between her teeth.

'I suggested passing time by playing chess, but he wanted something more relaxing, something he could do that wouldn't tax him, quite so much. He said he'd had a stressful day, and I thought he had a point.'

The finger touched her tongue. She tasted nicotine.

'So why not pop upstairs, I said. Won't she be asleep? he said. She might be, I replied, but that's a risk we've got to take. Anyway, I said, I doubt she'll mind. And even if she did, I said, it wouldn't really matter.'

He pulled the finger out. He slid it gently out. He eased his finger slowly out.

'So here we are,' he said, 'and off we go.'

He tugged the cord of the bedside lamp. A soft, unfocused light came on, a lilac glow which soothed them both, which made them calm before the storm. As ever Max was belted up, he was well and truly pulled in round the waist. He often let her choose which one he wore. He let her pick and choose her favourite piece of leather. He left the final outcome up to her. At least he had the decency to refuse to use the buckle, which left her free to concentrate on sifting different types of hide.

From time to time, depending on his mood,

he'd wrap the belt around his fist and make a show of asking what she wanted. He'd ask her what, precisely, she preferred, or how she'd care to be amused, or if she wished to be chastised. He told her it was called the Balkan Question.

Bruno stepped inside the room. He came towards the bed. The supple movements of a dancer as he slowly crossed the floor. Now she had them both. Max beside her, Bruno standing opposite. Hers and hers alone. She was the focus of their lives, the true and beating core of all they were, the sun that they revolved around.

Not bad, she thought, considering. She'd really done quite well. It could have turned out differently. She might have ended up in far less charming company, far less congenial surroundings. Not bad indeed, she thought, for surely there were bleaker ways of getting by, worse things on this earth, than lying, wet and waiting, on a bed in Little Venice.

'Bruno . . . ?'

When she said his name, pronounced it softly in the air, it sounded foreign, even to her foreign ear. The sweet, enticing promise of the way she breathed his name. He was standing, leaning slightly forward, his knee against the bottom of the mattress. He allowed himself to smile at her.

73

(Such teeth he had.) Already she had pleased them both, and the night had barely started.

'I don't know if I told you, I don't know if you've been informed, but it's my birthday,' Bruno said.

He wrapped his hands around her ankles. He held them in his newboy hands and gripped them fairly hard.

'I don't know if I mentioned it, but I'm the Birthday Boy.'

And having thus informed her of the current state of play, he pulled her legs apart. Though not too much. An inch or two, perhaps. (Or maybe three, she thought, for already she could think in inches.)

But however far he spread her legs, however much he opened them, it hinted there'd be more to come. That sudden, grasping movement, the clutching of the ankles, the way he gripped her with his Bruno-hands and pulled her legs apart – though not too much, an inch or two perhaps – it promised there'd be damper things to come. The way he did it boded well, reflected honour on his name, and showed he had the self-restraining virtue of the deeply vicious man.

'I think this might appeal to her,' Max said.

'I think you might be right.'

'It wouldn't appeal to everyone, but it might appeal to her.'

'She's not a very *normal* person.'

'To put it rather mildly.'

'And abnorms ought to stick together.'

'We can but try.'

Max removed his jacket. He held it up, and shook it once, then folded it, with some precision, across a Dralon chair. He seemed to take great pains with his appearance. He groomed himself, she felt, excessively. She watched his fingers fumble with the belt. The Moroccan one, she noted. Not quite the best, tonight, but mustn't grumble. A certain coarseness in the grain, but mustn't make a fuss. The Moroccan one would have to do.

Max held the silver buckle in his fist, and wrapped a length of supple leather once or twice around it.

'I wonder how she's feeling,' he remarked. Politely, yet without great interest, and apropos of nothing much.

How was she feeling? Enclosed, contained, immensely happy. How else should she feel, she thought. She turned and looked away. He didn't have to know it all. Not totally. Not absolutely everything.

She saw that Bruno understood. Bruno pressed against the bed and gazed at her. The Birthday Boy was gazing down. Some phrase escaped his lips, some murmured words that pulled his mouth apart but didn't reach her. He released his grip, and muttered quietly, perhaps for Max's benefit, and crossed his arms and gripped her ankles once again.

Before she'd realised what would happen, before she had a chance to brace herself, to savour the sensation, he flipped her over. The slightest flick of Bruno's wrists, and round she went. He turned her over, rotated her, showed her why he favoured revolution.

Her face was buried in the pillow, their *sotto voce* murmurs filled the room, their cryptic undertones and brief asides. And then they softly laughed, her darling boys. Perhaps it was the sight of her, the way they'd flipped her round, the spread of stockinged legs. It must have been amusing.

And when she felt a hand fold back the lace-edged slip, just roll it further up her back – but tenderly, with reverence – it came to her, quite forcefully, how glad she was to be in England, learning English ways.

The warm, Moroccan tongue of the chosen leather belt, it hardly brushed her skin, it barely touched the skin at all. She heard them move behind her in the room. There was an acrid smell, a whiff of sweaty expectation. The priests were slipping off their robes, about to worship at the altar.

Max bent down. He breathed hot breath against her neck, and touched her precious place. He held her head and pushed it even deeper in the pillow. She waited for the voice. She waited for the man to speak. She had to hear her master's voice.

A twenty-second lull, the briefest intermission, then he pressed his thin-lipped mouth against her ear, and whispered what they wanted. With unexpected urgency, describing pictures seen in some forbidden book, expressed in simple words that even she could understand, he told her what they'd do that night, the way they'd mark the birthday of the Birthday Boy.

'And whatever you might feel . . .'

He stroked her hair, kissed the skin behind her lobe.

'Whatever might occur, you must remember, finally, that all the things we do . . .'

He flexed the belt, kissed her once again.

'. . . are only done for you.'

9

In her more reflective moments, when they tired of being beastly and they left her to herself, she used to go from room to room and stroke the ornaments. She'd run her jealous fingers over objects he'd collected, and wonder why he valued them so much. Their tiny flaws, their surface imperfections, were vaguely disconcerting.

I've got those, she'd think. I'm flawed perfection too, she'd think. I'm yellowing with age, and I'm brittle with desire, but I'm not averse to having pleasure-spasms. For his jade and onyx statuettes had never quivered at his touch. They never trickled with delight, or begged the boys to stop, or shuddered in their sleep, or ached to be untied, or shrieked and sobbed and quietly bled. They never did a thing, she thought. It really wasn't fair.

She'd been tempted, on occasion. She'd had an urge to shatter what he cherished, destroy whatever might be irreplaceable. She wanted to express herself as cogently as possible, articulate her feelings in a way he'd understand. She'd fill a vase with golden piss, or lie down on the Persian rug and menstruate. She'd speak to him in private code. She'd say it with secretions.

Max caught her once. She'd lifted up a piece of porcelain, and held it high above her head, when in he came, the man himself, the object of the exercise.

'Being fretful, are we?'

He'd crossed the floor before she had a chance to move, before she could react, before she'd even blinked.

'Mustn't break what isn't ours.'

He grabbed her bony wrists, and plucked the dish away, and placed it on the mantelpiece.

'Mustn't vandalise, when one's in Little Venice.'

So the orifice was being rather uppity. The ever-dribbling ingrate didn't like his choice of *décor*. She'd have to learn some self-control. She'd have to learn to appreciate the finer things in life.

'If you tell me what's upsetting you, I'll try to put it right. I'll do my level best,' he said, 'I really, truly will,' he said, and bent her arms behind her back until they almost cracked, until they almost split apart, until she almost fainted with contentment.

'So tell me, while I'm asking. While I'm interested to know.'

With which enticing invitation, he released her. She rubbed her reddened skin and wondered how to phrase it most succinctly. She didn't want to miss the chance of oral interaction, and she pursed her lips and pondered, for a moment. The problem was, he'd got her far too cheaply: a piece of fruit, a slab of cheese, a pair of nylon knickers. Pleasure-spasms, now and then, of varied length and quality. The trouble was, the fundamental trouble was, she didn't cost enough to keep. She was disgustingly affordable.

'What I'd like,' she said, 'is spendables to squander. As you're asking,' she enlarged. 'And as you're keen to know.'

He barely flickered his dismay. He barely let it register. It seemed so pointless, suddenly. He'd always known she had this streak in her, this avaricious streak. So ingrained, by nature or by nurture, that he couldn't even beat it out. (Although, by God, he'd tried.) But this was how she was. She'd never *give* unstintingly. She couldn't let herself be gratified by seeing Maxie satisfied.

'If money's what you want,' he said, 'then money's what you'll get.'

(That word, he thought. She's made me use the money-word.)

She came up close and held him tight. She wrapped her sore and throbbing arms around him.

'You really mean it?' (Such hypocrites, they were. So soft and coy and caring.)

'Of course I do.' He kissed her on her self-deluding brow. 'I never lie to those I love.'

'When?' she urged, quite suddenly enthused.

'I'll discuss it with the paying guest. Take soundings, as it were.'

He poured himself a generous drink.

'But I do detect a *cooling* in the newboy's ministrations. A certain easing of his interest in your very charming self.'

A soda-spurt, to top it up, to make it froth and sparkle.

'So don't expect too much,' he smiled, 'and I'm sure we'll let you know.'

10

Bruno ran his fingers slowly down the shaft. He let his fingers linger on the short and stubby shaft. Just holding it excited him, filled him with exquisite potency.

'I think it's beautiful,' she said. 'I've always wanted one of those.'

He flushed with manly pride. She deserved a treat, he thought. He slipped a hand behind her neck, and pulled her head towards him. Mustn't be self-centred. Give the girl some happiness.

'Take a look at poetry.'

He pushed it in her face, and let her kiss the perfect tip. He let her wrap her painted lips around the polished tip. He loved it when he suckled her, those greedy sounds she made, completely unselfconscious. He could have stood and filled her mouth forever, but he didn't want to spoil her, he didn't want to let her have too much of it, too soon.

When, at length, he pulled it out, when he felt she'd had enough, and he gently slid it out, he saw she'd left a thin, transparent film around the end.

'You've made a mess,' he said, as she wiped it with her palm. Her liquids didn't seem to bother her, which was probably a healthy sign. She'd trickle either end, without complaint, without a break, without demanding sustenance of a more nutritious nature. A tremendous sport, he thought. She always played the game.

'Would Max mind me touching it?'

So tentative, she was, for she didn't want to break the rules, she knew decorum should prevail.

Bruno gave himself a moment to consider. Would Max mind, or would he not? He allowed himself to cogitate. He quietly mulled it over in his brain.

'He might,' he said, 'but if he does, he shouldn't. It shows you value what he loves.'

He held it in his hand. The hand-carved stock against his arm. The solid, savage heaviness. To hold and point a weight like that . . . no wonder it appealed.

'A stucco house, and inbred genes' – he held it to the light – 'and this.'

He touched the trigger with his thumb. He didn't press too hard. Just brushed it lightly with his thumb.

'The question surely is,' he said, 'has he ever used it? Has he ever raised this thing of his, this thick, truncated, sawn-off thing, in anger?'

He glanced at her, took in that placid, non-responsive face.

'Because if you're worried, if you're asking, if you'd really like to know, I'd say he hasn't.'

He regarded her again, and this time read her properly. He recognised the gaping need, and pushed the brutal shaft against her cheek.

'Max would disapprove of this.'

When he pushed the thing right in her face, she didn't seem to mind, she barely even flinched. But then she'd always been amenable. She wasn't one to make a fuss, if he recalled correctly.

'Max thinks girlies shouldn't play with guns.'

His finger on the trigger, and the barrels in her cheek. A sweaty boy from Willesden Green, it suited him to pose like that, to shove that stiffness in her face. (If you like them dark and gipsy, he's your man . . .)

He'd been drinking, which surprised her, for he didn't often drink. He wasn't one for swilling, of an evening. And when he held the sawn-off to her face, and moved his thigh between her legs, and breathed on her with whisky-breath, it surprised her even more, it suggested quite a different escalation. But even so, she wasn't too put out. The double-barrelled pressure wasn't too distressing.

'If you're good . . .' he said, 'if you behave . . .' he said.

'You'll what?'

'You'll see,' he said. 'Just wait.'

The edge was gone from him, that edge of edgy self-control which always held him back, was gone completely now. She had a sense that he might go too far, might even injure her, might blast her for the fun of it, might do her unimagined damage that couldn't be repaired. Where's Max, she thought.

'Where's Max?' she said.

She moved her face a fraction to the right, and stepped a half-pace forward, so that the barrel pressed more firmly, and his thigh was clamped more tightly. (In the absence of the host, this is how the guests will often interact.)

'He's gone to be examined.' The unaccustomed liquor smell. 'He's gone to let them poke around his privates.'

His mouth approached her ear.

'He thinks he might have picked up something nasty. Some germ that's working through his system, starting from his crotch.'

The famous Bruno zip came down, melodious and full of promise.

'I warned him it might happen, but did he listen? I told him what to do. Max, I said, you've got to wear a rubber. We don't know what she might have got. So keep your wits about you, and your whatsit clean. But did he listen? Did he?'

The weight of him, all gun and muscled thigh. Their foreheads touched, the barest mutual butting.

'And do we care?' His alcoholic breath against her face.

If his finger were to tighten on the trigger, if he had a Bruno-spasm and it tightened on the trigger, she wouldn't have to be there any more. If the spasm made him tighten, she'd be splattered on the wall. She'd be somewhere else entirely. She wouldn't be at all.

She wondered if her mouth were big enough, if she'd get it all to fit. She wondered whether she could part her coloured lips, and stretch them wide, and wrap them round the twin and glinting barrels of a double-barrelled shotgun.

He smiled, because he understood. He empathised completely. He shook his head, and sucked his teeth, and moved it down towards her neck. He gave a little nuzzle with the muzzle.

'You're aching for it, aren't you? Just waiting for a man like me to help you disappear.'

One day, he promised, if she asked him nicely, he might oblige and finish her. If she sprayed herself with jasmine scent, and rouged her cheeks, and wore that velvet dress, and didn't whine too much, and managed not to beg or plead, just asked him very nicely, he might well condescend to wipe her out.

But meanwhile, in the interim, he pressed her up against the wall, held the gun beneath her chin, moved the skirt six inches higher, pulled the cotton panties down, and pushed himself inside. (For the houseguest was a fairly pushy man.)

Opposite, there was an oval mirror. It looked expensive, hugely tasteful, quite beyond her reach. She observed herself, her curled and tinted hair spread out around her head, her narrow body nearly hidden, trapped behind the heaving Bruno back.

She was open-eyed with open admiration. That's me, she thought, and smiled at her reflection. He's doing that to me, she thought, and blew herself a large and silent kiss. She felt as though she were the centre of the cosmos, the focus of existence. She pulsed and throbbed with self-esteem, then suddenly came back to earth, and tried to let the liquid flow. But trying was so drying.

It wasn't Bruno's fault. She didn't really blame him, for the boy could only do his best. At least he had the grace to make the effort. But the mirror-image made her feel like some voyeur, as if she were a passer-by who'd wandered in, and now stood staring at a porno film, detached and coldly uninvolved. She watched the tiny movements that she always made, those sub-orgasmic shudders, those shivers of non-ecstasy, and whispered her endearments in his ear.

All of him was sweat, and thrust, and rigid concentration. He grunted as he tunnelled deep inside. Her only worry, that he might become so self-absorbed, so rampantly oblivious, that he'd spurt from every opening, forget himself and fire at her from every barrel. He knows me in and out, she thought, and laughed, although it wasn't that amusing, and of course he misconstrued, as the darlings always do. He stopped, and pressed his mouth into her neck, and took a fold of skin between his teeth. He bit it hard, then emptied hugely, like a whale.

The shotgun clattered to the floor and bounced against the skirting. He sagged against her, leaned his weight on top of her and crushed her up against the wall. She heard him groan, and felt him shrink inside. So long, she thought. Farewell, my little friend. He pulled away, and she felt it slither out. (A final gurgle as it left.)

She touched the bitten skin. That hurt, she thought. That bloody hurt. He was getting like the other one. Learning all his dirty tricks. She began to move aside and he grabbed her by the arm.

'Don't go,' he said.

'I've got to wash.'

'Don't wash.'

He took her by the elbow and led her into Max's private quarters, that special place to which they'd rarely been invited. (He'd found the key, of course. The newboy was quite sharp like that.) The room was almost free of any odour. Perspiration wasn't one of Max's weaknesses, and even what he spurted seemed to be unscented.

'Rosewood wardrobes,' Bruno said. 'Nothing but the best for Max.'

He pushed her forward, opened up the sliding doors.

Don't shut me in, she screamed. Don't leave me in the dark, I promise not to laugh again.

'Washing takes away the body's natural oils,' he said. 'Dries the skin and makes it flake. Wiping's always better.'

Silk and linen suits were hanging, colour-coded, on the right. The left-hand side was packed with floor-to-ceiling shelves, each of which contained a set of freshly-ironed under-wear. Bruno rummaged in a pile of thermal vests. He fished between the layers, and pulled out something suitable.

'Old men often wear this type of thing,' he said. 'Men like Max,' he said, and pulled her close.

'It stops them getting hypothermic.'

He lifted her skirt, a second time.

'Helps their circulation.'

He pressed the thermal vest between her legs, and began to wipe her clean. He gently rubbed the juice away, removed their freshly mingled mess, so she wouldn't have to wash on his account, and lose her natural body oils. He wrapped his arm still tighter round her waist and stroked her with an old man's vest. And as she counted up the circles that he made, she realised that she liked to have a Bruno looking after her. She rather liked the feel of thermal undies down below.

11

Max eased the Jag against the kerb. He switched off the ignition, and the engine died. They'd driven here for her. They'd get the girl some money, if that was what she wanted.

She shifted in her seat and squinted into the rain. She detested getting wet, if she could possibly prevent it. She loathed the thought of liquid on her skin. Even water gave her stress, these days, and apart from being bathed by Max, she avoided it completely. Apart from letting him explore his fetish for submersion, she avoided getting wet entirely.

She stared hard across the road. They were parked about fifty yards down from the garage. It would be over fairly quickly, or so the boys had promised. She merely had to bear in mind the things they'd said: remember not to talk too much, or to linger too long, or to come out running. (The latter, they had emphasised, was especially important.)

If she panicked, which they said they knew she wouldn't, but if she did, they pointed out – grinning as they twisted pale and fragile arms behind her back – if her lack of moral fibre sent her screaming down the road, she'd wish she hadn't met them, they'd make her rather sorry, they'd make her rue the day she'd found a bed in Little Venice.

It was good of them to let her know. Big of them to warn her. Decent of her undemanding boys to caution her beforehand, impress upon her not to let them down. For of all the fears she had in life, the greatest was her fear that she might one day let them down.

So having coached her carefully, having drummed the message home, having bent her dainty arms behind her back, they piled into the car and sped off down the road. And here they were, at last. Parked and silent by the kerb. Max doused the lights, and they watched the windows steaming up. Here they were, the three of them, the loving little troika.

She squirmed inside the coat. She wrapped its cashmere folds around her, and strained to hear the nearly-silent ticking of the clock. She was very partial to that car, very much a Jag

aficionado. She often had a sense of almost athe-
istic exaltation when she sat there with her dress
rolled up, and felt the friction of her precious
place against the hand-stitched hide.

Contentment, she soon realised, lay in bounc-
ing on a sculpted leather seat, while Bruno
sniggered in the rear, and tight-lipped Max went
slicing down the road.

But not tonight, of course. Tonight was rather
different. Tonight she'd had the grace, indeed
the foresight, to ensure she wore the usual
undergarments. (In any case, they protected her
from chills, and had the great advantage of
conforming to what other women did.)

'You're expecting me to go in there?'

She sounded unusually alert, Max thought, as
if the brain she had, the only one He'd blessed
her with, were functioning correctly, for a
change. The concentration of her intellect, the
mental effort emanating from her cranium, was
almost palpable. For once she wasn't thinking
with her creamy bits. She wasn't just a pair
of juicy lips, he realised. Or not entirely, anyway.

'In there,' she said, 'is where you want me?'

'It is,' Max said.

How quick she was, he mused. How keenly-
honed the mind.

'Just pop across the road, and sidle through

the forecourt, and slip inside the shop. Just step inside and do your stuff.'

He glanced at Bruno in the mirror.

'But a word of caution, should you be receptive: I think you'll find the man behind the till, the man who takes the punters' cash, a somewhat unengaging type. Not lovable, alas. Not like newboy and myself.'

'What's wrong with him?'

There was a slight, seductive note of mutiny, a suggestion that she might not see it through, she might decide to cut and run.

'Nothing too spectacular. Nothing too emetic.'

Max hurried to placate. He rushed to calm her down.

'But he's got these wart-like growths on both his thumbs, which he scratches under stress. So don't fraternise, is how I'd put it. Don't let yourself make friends with him. Don't be too obliging, is what I'd like to say.'

He bared his teeth and smiled.

'In case he tries to finger you, I mean. Remember why you're there, and step up to the till, and smile at him, and gently stroke his thumbs, and ask him for the money.'

'Ask him nicely,' Bruno added.

He was sprawling right behind her. He'd spread himself across the seat, and allowed himself to sprawl.

'Politeness often helps, I've always found. And if, by chance, it doesn't, show him your enormous thing. Let him see it glisten in the light. Just take it out, and let him have a look, let him gaze in adoration. You never know,' he murmured, 'you might be pleasantly surprised.'

'Should I let him touch it?'

There she went again, they thought. The little tease, the rank *provocateuse*.

Max peered into the gloom. He hoped she wouldn't try to aggravate. She had this streak in her, this tiresome streak, this constant inclination to enrage, until they had that leaping urge, that pure and throbbing need, to punish her.

'Look,' he said, 'it might not interest you, as such, but all of this is down to Bruno. This little expedition, this jolly evening jaunt, this hopeful sally in the dark, is all because of him. He thought it might be rather droll to let you have your head. A brief and fleeting moment of significance. A liberating minute when the walls come tumbling down. Catharsis in North Kensington.'

He swallowed down what might have been a sneer.

'Empowerment of the masses, I think he called it. Namely you, I think he meant. One trusts you follow, and if you do – any questions?'

She pondered deeply for a second. She puckered up her unlined brow and contemplated, for an instant.

'So can I let him touch it, then?'

'Better not.'

(Bruno, from the rear.)

'He won't respect you once he's touched it, and I think you want respect.'

'I think I do,' she said.

Max wiped the windscreen clear with a battered leather driving-glove. Dusk was beginning to fall, and a line of orange streetlamps flickered on.

'Once you've got the lot,' he said, 'once he's made his contribution to the cause of refugees, just come outside and walk off down the road. Don't look back, and please don't run.'

Pause for manly snigger.

'Little girlies always draw attention when they run, and we don't want that, my love. We don't want to see you running off, and getting caught, and put inside.'

He grinned at his reflection.

'That's not exactly what we want.'

He twisted round in the driver's seat, his loose mouth open, the soft lips primed and ready.

'She wouldn't care for it, I think.'

He very nearly spurted when he thought of what would happen, the unexpected practices she'd have to entertain.

'All those pervs and sadists. All those retards. All night long.'

'And then there's the prisoners,' Bruno added. 'They'll want some too.'

Max shook his head regretfully.

'She's not a prison *type*, one fears. They wouldn't *indulge* her, I'm afraid.'

'And she does so like to be indulged.'

'She does.'

'They'll do horrid things in hidden rooms, and when she's served her time she'll be expelled. It'll all have been for nothing.'

'But she'll have had the experience.'

'She will, which can't be bad.'

Such boys they were, such brave and generous boys. They revelled in the knowledge that they'd helped a girl in need, they'd given her sensations which would stay with her forever. But it was time to let her go. It was time to cut the cord and let their baby go.

Max leaned across and shoved against the door. An ice-cold gust of air knifed inside the car.

'I suppose you'd better start,' he said, 'you'd better do your bit.'

His rotting gut, his Maxie breath, came blowing in her face.

'Just don't be long, is all I'd like to add.' And he pushed her smoothly out.

She stood and shivered on the pavement. Sleet

was falling in diagonal flurries. Her stomach was empty, and she felt sick with excitement. She pulled on the unworn gloves. Soft and black and tight, a thoughtful gift from the man she loved. She pictured him, the weight of him, the warm and newboy scent of him, and brushed her frozen lips with a suede-encircled finger.

An overloaded lorry churned through the unsalted slush. She watched it slowly pass, then slipped across the road. The traffic wasn't heavy, which came as no surprise, for no one lingered on the street on a wretched night like that. They had the sense to keep indoors, to lie beneath their cotton sheets and stroke themselves to sleep.

They didn't leave the boys behind and watch a lorry trundle past. They stayed inside their stinking homes. They stayed at home and stank. They didn't lick a scrap of silk-lined suede, and trot across the road, and wonder if they'd dare to let their precious thing, their pure and sacred happiness, be fondled by a man with warty thumbs.

The pumps were gleaming on the empty forecourt. The petrol-shop looked invitingly bright. She almost thought it seemed to wait for her, she almost fancied it expected her, she half-imagined that it quietly beckoned to the girl from Budapest.

She pushed open the plate-glass door. The man behind the till, the huge and heartless money-man, allowed himself a furtive glance, a modest ogle of approval. He even winked at her, and smacked his fatman's lips together. But she didn't mind. She understood.

Let him get his pleasures while he can. Let him feast his piggy eyes on quality.

A quite colossal brute, she noted, with distended cheeks and a slightly puckered, moistly anal, mouth. Vulgar-looking, as Max might well have said. Coarse, to be precise. A man who'd gone to seed, and sat there taking punters' cash, and sometimes did unpleasant things beneath the counter.

The shelves were stacked with cans of oil and rubber mats, and substances of different kinds to pour inside one's car. (Not to mention burgers to be microwaved, and sandwiches and chocolate bars. All that one might ever need for a fairly wholesome life.)

She chose a bag of barley sugar, and moved towards the well-built man, the man with famous growths. He was sitting, watching, mutely sweating. Behind him, through an open door, she glimpsed a large, soot-grey Alsatian. It was lurking, more than prowling. Dribbling, more than drooling.

A smell came wafting over her, that pungent,

cheesy smell of unwashed bits and bobs, that unmistakable odour that often taints the air. The reek of it. The ripe and brazen stench. A spot of gelding might not go amiss. Dog and master both, she felt, and smiled across at the unsmiling man.

Fluorescent light came pulsing from the ceiling. It bounced off the high-gloss walls, and hummed and quivered inside her head. She gazed at the man – at his rectal mouth, and his venal face – and wondered if she would have wanted him, if she might have let him touch her tender places with his thick and warty fingers, had he only been astute enough to reside in Little Venice.

He placed his hand on the cellophane packet and slid it towards him.

'We sell a lot of these,' he said, and rang up something silly on the till. 'Anything else?

His saliva-bubbles formed and burst, and for a single, fleeting second, she imagined that the thing beneath her coat was getting warmer, pinkly glowing in advance, heating up in readiness. It almost felt as if her mute and silent implement were throbbing with excitement, pulsating in suspense. She sniffed the scented air and stared at him.

So ugly, he was. So malformed the face. So shining the urge to smash it. It made her wonder if a man like that, a grotesque man with a genital stench (to give the dog, for once, the benefit of the doubt), could transform and reinvent himself, refine his speech, acquire a velvet stool, and drape her fragrant form across it.

'Is there anything else?'

Twin halogen beams swung on to the forecourt, and a dark and low-slung shape crawled up to the air pump. She watched the headlights dim. The driver climbed out, and bright shards of percussive jazz came beating through the night.

How many baths she would have to endure, how clean she would have to be, how diligently scrubbed her flesh, how obliging to her boys, to afford a car like that.

'You want something else?

She turned back to the man. This was the moment, the succulent moment. The boys had prepared her well, instructed her in what to say, and told her how to say it. They'd beaten in the script until she almost bled, so she didn't want to let them down. But suddenly the words she'd learned, those honeyed words they'd drilled into her skull, just wouldn't leave her mouth. She couldn't even spit them out, had she cared to be so gross.

'What do you want, love?'

Be honest with him, she told herself. Give it

to him straight. Allow this unappealing oaf to glimpse your inner essence.

'I want money,' she said.

Her enunciation pleased her. It was clear, and almost uninflected. She had spoken the simple line with the merest hint, the barest suggestion, of an intriguingly mitteleuropean accent.

She glanced up at the security camera. Its unblinking, electronic eye was watching her, and she sucked in her cheeks to accentuate the Slavic bones. She would be caught on film, captured for posterity, immortalised in black and white.

She looked back at the man. Such a pointless man.

'The money,' she clarified, 'is what I want.'

He shrugged, completely unperturbed, comprehension quite eluding him. She realised that he didn't understand. The moron didn't get it.

'Everyone wants money,' he said.

'I know they do.'

She gave him an encouraging smile.

'But I want *your* money.'

He was freakishly large, that man. Monumentally huge. He would have dwarfed Max, or even Bruno, had they stepped inside, had they come in from the rain and stood beside him. There were bigger men around, it seemed, than her favourite pair of wastrels.

He pulled out a shiny wallet and flipped it open.

'How much do you want?'

She watched him remove a selection of distressingly grubby notes. This did seem an exceptionally promising start. No pleading, no whining, no pressing secret panic-buttons, of which the boys had warned her.

'How much have you got?' she asked. Magnanimity might be called for. She needn't take it all, for she'd never been a greedy type. Or not excessively, she felt.

'Depends on what you do,' he said. 'You earn it, and you'll get it.'

'That's true,' she murmured.

'Tell you what, my love . . .'

He placed his meaty forearms on the counter and peered at her. He sized her up, mentally undressed her, and made a rapid calculation in his head.

'Seeing as it's Friday, and as I'm feeling generous, and as you've shown what might be called initiative, which is something I admire,' he said, 'here's five . . .'

He laid the note down on the polished beige Formica.

'. . . and we'll have a quickie.'

All brawn and belly. Wartiness personified. Reek and stench and puckered lips.

'Just the two of us, that is.'

He breathed kebab-breath in her face, and nodded over his shoulder.

'And my dog.'

An explosion came out of his mouth, an oral breaking of wind, a tiny, tongue-shaped fart that she recognised as an attempt at laughter.

'Love me,' he insisted, 'love my dog.'

Max would, no doubt, have termed it a necessary escalation, but even Max, she thought, surely not even Max, she thought . . .

'Fair enough,' she said.

She leaned forward slightly, and lowered her voice, making him strain to hear the words.

'But the dog goes first.'

A tremor passed across his face, a brief and uncontrollable spasm. (I get those, she thought. I get spasms.) For one ecstatic moment, she was sure he would lunge at her and clutch her with his massive hands. For a single, hideous instant, she expected him to heave his eighteen stone across the counter and wrap his stubby hands around her neck, her fragile stem, and squeeze it fairly hard, perhaps until it snapped.

She stood there, tensed and waiting, not unwilling, but he didn't move. With manly self-control, he resisted the temptation, he let it pass him by. The blob refused to blink.

'I think I don't much care for you, my darling.'

He said the words regretfully. More in sorrow, than in anger.

'Why ever not?'

'I'm not sure how to put it.'

'Don't mind me,' she said.

'If I can be quite honest, then . . .'

'You can.'

'You're absolutely sure . . . ?'

'I am.'

His tongue flicked out and travelled round his lips. He moistened them, to smooth the words, to ease their passage out.

'Frankly speaking then,' he said, 'I think you're what one tends to call a cunt.'

She gazed at him with some distaste. Reprovingly, in fact. Not just coarse of feature, but coarse of mind and soul.

'No, darling.'

She reached inside her coat, and touched her hidden preciousness. She let her hand embrace her quietly waiting core. It was then she realised, with rare and perfect insight, that every girl should have one. Let him see how blessed she was. Let him drool with envy. Let him only wish he had the same.

'That's not entirely accurate,' she said.

She pulled out her glorious thing.

'I'm a cunt with a sawn-off shotgun.'

She thumbed back the hammer, and pointed the barrels at his bovine face.

'And I really, truly, badly want your money.'

The bliss of it. The glory. The life-enhancing grandeur of her grandest-ever moment. For here she was, a piece of foreign flotsam far from home, a mute, illegal entrant in this land, yet still she had the strength of mind to reach inside her cashmere coat and bring out something brutal. If Bucharest could only see her now . . .

She moved it slowly forward, until the smoothly bevelled end, the very tip of all she had, and all she'd ever need, was pressing gently up against his mouth.

At her polite request, he allowed his jaw to sag, and let her slip her gleaming thing inside. She eased it past the soft and pliant lips, and felt a tiny quiver, a barely tangible vibration, as it knocked against his teeth.

'Won't be long,' she promised.

She held her suede-gloved finger on the trigger, and jammed the weapon in. She rammed it well and truly in.

'Just a quickie,' she added, and watched, with mild detachment, as liquid from his loose and gaping hole ran down the well-oiled shaft.

12

She backed carefully out of the door. It hadn't
lasted long. The boys were right, as usual. Being
hugely brainy boys, they'd always get it right.
She backed out rather slowly, encumbered, as
she was. Weighed down with chocolate bars,
and bags of hard-boiled sweets, and mentho-
lated cigarettes, and crumpled banknotes by the
score, and unused cartridges, and sawn-off
guns. The pick of all the goodies on this vast,
abundant earth.

She had left him standing, hands on head,
behind the till. She felt it showed she empathised. It showed she had a human side, a tender,
beating heart beneath the palpitating flesh. But
she'd warned him not to move, she'd told him
what would happen if he had the gall to move.
She'd pressed her awesome thing against his

face, and advised him not to shift, if he could possibly avoid it.

When she saw that he believed her, when she saw that what she said was rather plausible, she realised that she'd solved her basic problem, she's found the final answer to her lack of credibility. She wished she'd thought of it before, indeed wondered why she hadn't. For a woman in a cashmere coat, with a hard and shining thing, would always get respect. She'd always be the centre of attention.

Once outside, she walked across the forecourt, and kept on walking down the road. The boys had told her not to run, and she obeyed them, even now. She was listening to her masters' voice as it led her down the road.

Those two, she thought. They must be getting bored, these days. They might insist on something quite outrageous. She considered what she might be called upon to do that night, the escalations necessarily inflicted. And then she pictured all the money that she carried, the thousands that the loose-lipped man had given her. And then she thought again of what they might demand of her, and she realised that she didn't have to do it, any more. She didn't have to let the boys amuse themselves, if she didn't really want to.

And she recognised, with quite liberating clarity, that she really didn't want to.

She stopped to catch her breath, and stared towards the car. They were sitting, waiting, in the dark. Holding what she'd gained that night in a pair of plastic bags, she leaned against a wall and watched the silent car. She knew they must be squinting through the gloom to try and catch a fleeting glimpse of foreign girly, and so trained she was, her reactions so Pavlovian, that she almost crossed the road towards them, she almost stepped out from the shadows and ran across the road.

But when she felt it once again – the sawn and polished pair of tubes, her quite enormous implement – she knew that happiness was leaving her admirers in the rain. Happiness was packing grubby banknotes in a bag, and leaving Max and Bruno wilting in the rain. She'd earned it, after all. By the law of finders-keepers, it was hers. So without a backward glance, and with her future in her hands, she left them in the dark and walked away.

Already, they were fading in her mind. Their overwhelming presence slowly shrivelled in the memory. She didn't want them, any more. She didn't even need them. They were nothing very special. There was nothing there at all. She carried all she'd ever wished for in some tattered plastic bags, and she'd never have to let them, any more. Up in heaven, angels sang and bells rang to mark the auspicious moment. For there are two kinds of women in this world: those with money, and those without. Not the virgin and the whore, but the wealthy and the poor.

She pushed open a heavy, oak door and stepped inside. There seemed to be too many of them, packed tight together, enveloped in a fug of smoke, pressed up against each other in the orange-hued warmth. The place stank of bodies and damp clothes and she felt immediately at home.

She shouldered her unassuming way between the gaps, excusing herself when she trod on someone's foot, as she did, from time to time. She smiled, though not excessively. Politely, as appropriate. The way you do when you push past drinking men in a tight-packed winter pub. Their beer-breath filled the air, and snatches of what passed for conversation ebbed and flowed around her.

Occasionally, a gleeful, sodden face would turn to her, she'd see an open hole with froth around its lips, a pink and shining tongue that curled and swelled inside, and hear some sound come out, some farmyard noise, some aural indication of testosterone.

'You all right then?'

She turned and saw a grinning man observing her, his proud, possessive arm around a gaunt-faced female, fifty-odd and ageing fast. Good-will came off him in waves, transparent decency and neighbourly concern. A thigh lightly touched her own, and there was a shyly flabby growth between his legs.

His leather blouson jacket seemed at macho odds with the soft and formless face. He looked the type who didn't have to shave too often, the pink-skinned, hairless type who couldn't hold his liquor, who only fought when in a pack, and still believed he was a man. A wave of misanthropic rage engulfed her, and she felt a kind of non-specific warmth for Max, who alone would understand.

'Cheer up, love,' the woman said. 'It might never happen.'

Her eyebrows had been plucked away to nothing, as if she were some mutant doll, some throwback to the Forties. The thin and pencilled lines drawn high above the bone, the drinker's face and smoker's teeth, and every single time she spoke, the tiny ball of spit that issued from her mouth.

The girl from Bratislava could have given her another hole, she could have pointed at the woman's head and blown it half away. Gouged out a fresh and gaping wound, with charred and ragged edges. She could have gladly done it, had she had the time.

The man was pale and thin, defeat ingrained in every pore. The girl imagined how he'd be that night, spreading out those brittle limbs, resting on his woman like a desiccated leaf. Breathing halitosis in her face, while she lay grunting underneath and let herself be taken by a dull and weightless man. For even one like that, even one who lacked the weight to keep her prone beneath him, was an altogether better bet than none at all.

The girl, the armed and vicious foreigner, smiled a gentle, Balkan smile. Suddenly she wished to finish them, to send them sagging to the floor. If I were you, she nearly said, I'd kill myself. I'd lie down in a steaming bath and open up my veins. That's what I'd do, if I were you.

'Sorry, but I've got to dash. I'm afraid I really must.'

She slid demurely past the happy couple.

'My boys,' she murmured, and pushed her furtive way a little deeper into the room.

A pair of wooden booths were tucked into the corner, secluded from the throng. Behind the booths, a door. And stencilled on the door an outline to enchant: a male without unsightly bulges, a pre-pubescent little chap, without unfortunate appendages.

She didn't think she'd ever been inside one, in the past. Nor had she ever had the inclination. She'd never had the privilege to step inside the holy sanctum, where the priestly caste would congregate and fling admiring glances at each other's infantilia.

A row of porcelain urinals – probably Victorian, and probably quite valuable – stretched against the furthest wall. A gutter stained a citrus-yellow ran their length, and carried off the golden nectar, removed it to some better place.

The single male inside was standing, legs apart, intent and happy at his task. The sturdy shoulders were broad and pin-striped, the shoulders of a man who'd weathered the recession, who'd paid off his debts and could piss with pride.

Being blessed with weaponry, being loaded down with unearned dosh and therefore keen to make an entrance, she slammed the door as she stepped inside. She let the heavy door bang shut behind her.

The quietly flowing businessman (whose name was Don) half-turned to see who'd come to join, which fellow member of the scrotal class was about to stand beside him.

There was a moment's incredulity, and then the paralysing recognition that he was totally alone, bereft of all assistance, abandoned in a lavatory, unzipped and bare, his warm and much-loved preciousness – his micturating hope and joy – oblivious and pumping hard, while a female sidled neatly past, a demented grin spread on her face and a sawn-off in her hand.

13

Through the door, and out into the yard, and the cold air felt raw on her face. It rubbed her pallid skin until it almost bled, and made her breath condense before her eyes. Here she was, a nobody, a mute and nameless refugee in the bleak and empty space behind the pub. She shivered with dismay, for she had nothing, in this world, but a small yet perfect fortune and a fully-loaded shotgun.

She walked towards the road. Down an alley and out into the road. She couldn't help but chuckle to herself, a slightly manic yet endearing sound that bubbled up from deep within. (Although to someone else's ears, to someone reared in gentler ways, to someone born with spendables, it might have seemed offensive.)

She couldn't help but salivate, as she trotted

down the road. She thought of what she'd done, and the boys she'd left behind. And how the petrol-man had looked, when she looked him in the eye. And the money, and the glory, and the God-denying thrill of it.

She broke into a run, an unathletic slither, and as she turned a corner slipped on ice, and fell down hard. She fell, in fact, without finesse. Not knowing how to do it gracefully, she banged on to the pavement. She bruised an elbow, grazed her temple and, to cap it all, was sure she'd soon begin to menstruate, which didn't help. (She always felt so nauseous, so thoroughly hormonal. Roll on the menopause, she was often prone to think.)

She sat there, for a moment, on the wet and icy pavement, then touched her swollen knee and hobbled on. It was difficult to walk, and it hurt her, quite excessively. Each step she took, she took in pain. But even so, even though her leg began to throb and her head began to ache, she knew she'd found tranquillity. She'd found contentment, on this earth. She'd found the pure, unsullied freedom of the rich and well-respected.

By the time she'd covered four more blocks, the sleet had thinned to a scattered rain, and the slush was disappearing. She heard the car, before she saw it. Perhaps she sensed it, before she heard it. The familiar phallic shape pulled in, a yard or two ahead of her. It eased into the pavement, nudged against the kerb, glided to a stop.

Someone shoved the rear door open, and it completely blocked her path. The inside light came on, and there the darlings were. They'd come for her, as she knew they would. They'd come to fetch her home.

She only had to see them both, and she felt the usual pang. She felt nostalgia overwhelm her, although she'd barely been away. To see them was to want them, to feel oneself begin to lubricate, to make one's panties sodden with expectancy.

'Hello boys,' she said.

Max sat quietly brooding at the wheel, affecting not to care, as if she couldn't smell the damply urgent need that sweated from his every pore. The other one, the Bruno-one, had spread himself, quite fetchingly, across the leather seats.

She gazed with undiminished admiration at the two of them, her cherished pair of priapists, and allowed the barrel of her thing to poke demurely from her coat. She thought again of what she'd done a while ago, the joys of interacting in that very special way, and recognised how much she yearned to do it, once again.

'Remember this?' she said, and pulled it out completely, exposed it to the elements, revealed her pride and pleasure to the lads. It suited her, she felt, tremendously. A chic and stubby counterpoint to what she knew she was. She held the now-familiar weight and levelled it at the top, the very crown, of Bruno's head.

The latter, to his credit, barely blinked. Supremely self-controlled, prepared to stare her out, he merely shifted his position, minutely rearranged his facial muscles. Perhaps there was a twitch below the eye, but she really couldn't tell. It might have been imagination, wishful thinking on her part, the fond, unlikely fancy of an over-active orifice. For such was what she knew she was. She'd attained a state of heightened self-awareness, and recognised what others couldn't face: when all was said and done, she had a basic need for certain kinds of friction. A mutual bonding of the lower parts. Some rubbing and some grubbing.

'Shall I take that?'

Bruno had pronounced, at last. He uttered solemn words, and pricked her self-obsessive bubble.

'Why don't you let me have it?'

The soft and soothing tone, the gently rampant tenderness.

'It's mine,' she said.

'I know it is.'

'It belongs to me.'

'Of course it does.'

'I haven't even fired it yet.'

(She managed not to whine, but only just.)

'Another time, perhaps,' the newboy said. 'Why don't you let me have it?' he repeated, perhaps a trifle rashly. 'Just hand it over, and get inside, and I'll let you suck that bit you love.'

His hand approached his newboy crotch.

'Why don't I keep it,' she replied. 'And you can suck that bit yourself.'

On hearing which profound remark, Max twisted round to get a better look. This, he felt, was something new. This was something that could well be termed a novelty. This was what transpired when girlies played with guns.

He shuddered at the sight of her. His privates quailed with horror. They quietly shrivelled with distaste. Be gentle with the bitch, he thought. Be patient with the unhinged little sow.

'Look,' he said, placatingly. 'We want to help. We really do. Just tell us what the problem is, and we'll try and sort it out.'

Fair point, she thought. What exactly *was* it that was needling her? What burden seemed to fill her life and weigh her down? What was it that annoyed her, most of all?

She cogitated, for a moment, and then enlightenment arrived. That's it, she thought. That's really it. No wonder she'd been feeling glum.

'You're sure you want to know?'

'We are,' they chimed, in unison.

'Well I'm sick of being fucked.'

The heresy sank home. There were manly grunts of disapproval. Snorts of disbelief. Total incredulity. She must have flipped her tiny lid. She must be quite insane.

'You're being quite ridiculous.'

Max was simply horrified. This had surely gone beyond a joke. He'd have to put her right. Remind her of the facts of life.

'You *know* you enjoy it.'

'But I'm *sick* of enjoying it.'

Bruno, at whose head the loaded gun was pointing, felt he ought to try and bring things to some kind of resolution.

'Look' he said. 'Be good,' he said. 'We'll talk it over once you're in the car.'

He smiled, to show he empathised.

'You can keep the money.'

She moved a step towards him. He'd let her keep her gains. A kind and generous man. Firm yet fair. And handsome, too.

'All of it?' (Her constant tendency to wheedle.)

'The lot,' he said.

Sometimes women love their chains. They want to feel them tight around their wrists. They want to bend the knee, and kiss the glory of the master. Even when they've got a shooter in their hands, they get this urge to hand it back, to give it up to someone else, and let him help them climb inside. Some girls don't deserve a gun.

'Can I really keep the money?'

He kissed her trembling cheek, and leaned across and pulled the car door shut behind her. Max floored the accelerator. There was a smell of burning rubber, and the Jag took off at speed.

'You nearly shot me,' Bruno said.

'You don't know that. You can't be sure.'

'It was written on your face, my love.'

He pulled her forward, right across his knees. He pressed her down across his lap and slid a hand beneath the skirt.

'To think of all we've done for her. The joy we've gladly given. The total satisfaction.'

His ruminating hand beneath the skirt.

'It's time to teach her some respect.'

Max headed towards Lisson Grove. They'd show her what was what. They'd make her understand the way things really were. So she's sick of being fucked, he thought. Good grief, whatever next?

As he headed down the Grove, he heard that

special sound she made, that foul and dirty pleasure-sound, that semi-gurgle in her throat. He changed down into third and took a bend. The engine screamed. That's right, old mate, you teach her.

Bruno, somewhat self-absorbed, and with one hand on her neck, unpeeled her charcoal tights. He rolled them slowly down, stopping just above her knees, so that they formed a kind of binding round her legs. She struggled, in a desultory fashion, but he had the grace to hold her down. Even though she'd aimed her loaded thing at Bruno's head, he had the decency to hold her firmly down.

Her face half-buried in the hide, she felt obscurely comforted that life as she had known it, the tiny slice they'd granted her, had resumed its normal course. The structures were in place again, and the boys were back in town.

'One day you'll thank us, sweetheart.'

The gentle Bruno murmur in her ear.

'Thank you, boys, you'll say. I needed that, you'll add. You're bound to thank us, one fine day. But perhaps not yet, one fears.'

He hooked a warm, familiar thumb beneath the tight elastic. (Mine, he thought. All mine.)

'One day, you'll be so grateful . . .'

He eased the cotton panties halfway down her thighs.

'. . . but not quite yet, I think.'

And he placed a contemplative hand on the pink and stateless rump.

14

Max opened his eyes in the dark.

An obscure and intangible fear had entered his dream and jerked him awake, some dim and shapeless sense of threat that pressed upon his sluggish brain and forced it back to consciousness. His head felt raw from lack of sleep, as if they'd sliced it open, split it like a coconut, and now were standing peering in, about to touch and fondly prod. The air had that smell of dead of night, those empty hours when normal people, wholesome types who paid their bills and lived in suburbs, slept and rubbed and quietly oozed.

He grimaced as a minute patch, a soft and tender fold of discreetly sweating skin, began to itch. His mind, which always darted on ahead, which ran to meet misfortune, conjured up a vision of his lower parts, his moistly helpless nether regions, bursting out with cysts and running sores, while polyps flowered by the score, and blisters swelled and gently split.

'Multicoloured secretions,' he murmured, 'and modest suppurations.'

He ran his tongue around his mouth, and moved his hand and scratched himself. He hoped he hadn't woken them. They deserved their sleep, he thought. A well-earned rest was theirs by right.

He scraped a sharpened fingernail across the agitated skin. Might only be a rash, he reasoned. A touch of prickly heat. He scraped a little harder. She didn't look infectious, although one couldn't really tell. He should have had her tested, at the start. He should have had her checked out right away. The itch was slowly getting worse, and he hoped he wouldn't wake them as he scratched and softly groaned.

He listened to their breathing: in and out, and out and in. It ebbed and flowed around him. He recognised, quite suddenly, how blessed he was, how reassured, to hear them breathing in the dark, to hear the womb-like sounds they made while splayed and helpless on his bed.

Hers were barely audible, but Bruno's had that certain Bruno style. Even in his sleep, even with their vaguely mucoid undertone, they had a kind of smothered strength, as if some god were sprawled beside him, and not a mortal man. Bruno spread out on the bed. Bruno breathing on the bed. Max touched himself, removed the droplet which had formed, and wiped his fingers on the sheet. He stared ahead, his eyes adjusting to the gloom.

Now and then a car went past, and he'd watch the headlights chase across the wall. His head was mildly throbbing and his gut began to ache. That wine, he thought, that Bruno wine. The cheap, red wine the guest had bought was churning in his belly, stagnating deep inside. They wanted him to rot away. They wanted him to putrefy. He'd let a pair of grinning thieves inside his home, and now they'd wormed their parasitic way inside his bed, and pressed their leeching mouths against his skin, and tried to suck him dry.

He touched himself, again. He held himself, quite tenderly. Those scum, he thought, that pair of sluts, those self-indulgent slimes. Those insects curled beneath his sheets. He was their wallet, couch and feeding-trough. Tears pricked his eyes. He loved himself so much. (His goodness, in particular.) He wept and wallowed in the dark, and stroked his pure and upright pride, he pulled and rubbed and played with it, until it gushed with gratitude.

Moans and groans and clotted sheets.

But the very thought of them, of what he did and didn't do and what he let them get away with nearly spoiled it all. It nearly spoiled the satisfaction of his auto-interaction. For he paid them, fed them, often watched them fornicate, and even when they laid her down, and stretched her out, and went in either end – then gravely swapped positions like a pair of village cricketers – he always felt, however good it was, however generous she had been, that Bruno, being Bruno, had the best of her. Max always seemed to get the dregs, the residue of what was left, while she herself, the ever open aperture, had begun to make demands.

Nothing too explicit. Not insisting, just implying. As if the marks he gave her weren't enough. As if to be his chosen one, the one on whom he vented his disgust, the single one, in all the world, on whom he wished to spurt, were somehow insufficient.

The Bruno-wine was silting up his stomach, and he felt a fair-sized burp, a manly belch, erupting through his windpipe. He opened his mouth and released some gas, then breathed it, sweetly stinking, back into his nose. What came out went in again. Everything recycled, in the perfect eco-system.

He chuckled quietly in the dark, and felt her

move beside him. The heat of her, the fleshy, waiting warmth. He thought of them, and felt himself begin to mellow. Perhaps they weren't so bad, when all was said and done. Perhaps they weren't so terrible, as random bedmates went. He thought of her and Bruno. He pictured them, the pair of them, insistent movement in the dark. He thought of her, he thought of him, he thought of them together. He felt himself emerge again, ready for the fray. He gripped the freshly throbbing root and held it tight. Some life, he thought, some bloody life: middle-aged and pumping hard, clasping in his sweaty hand the thing he valued most on earth.

Staring up at nothing, he tried to recall her voice, but its precise tone, its exact quality, eluded him. He knew that she sounded endearingly coarse. That much, at least, he remembered. She'd somehow learned demotic speech, delivered at a grating pitch. And she tried, which only made it worse, for in Max's universe, in Max's coldly unforgiving cosmos, there were never points for trying. It was infinitely aggravating. The sound, alone, provoked him. That voice she had, that wheedling, female, fuck-me voice.

Perhaps that was why, in his more forbearing moments, when self-control was uppermost and he managed to refrain from pushing all he had inside her mouth, as men in Little Venice often do, he preferred to wrap a gag around her face. He'd bind her mouth and shut her up, which seemed an act of almost saintly self-restraint. (To him, that is, if not to her.)

He'd place a piece of tape across her lips, and press it down. That was what he often did, these days. He found he had this constant need to silence her. It was his tendencies, his honest inclinations, that made him. She understood, at least. An understanding woman. A great capacity to *empathise*, he mused. She had her merits, her oiled and open virtues, her gaping sensitivities. But still a dreadful shame about the voice.

Even so, he told himself, it had worked out well. Sometimes when, despite themselves, they made her happy – when they did their joyful business and worked her well and truly over, as good friends well and truly should, and she lay there clamped between them making sated, shameless noises, when she filled the room with sow-like grunts, quite heedless of the neighbours – sometimes, when that happened, which from time to time it did, he'd think how glad he was, how touched and truly grateful, to have found such friends as these.

We few, he'd think, we happy few . . .

Him and her and Bruno, all together. Her and

him, and him and Bruno. The mutual friction of their mutual friendship.

He sighed a sigh of expectation and rolled on to his hip. The bed, a massive slab of hand-carved maple, creaked and dipped beneath him. He moved his hand to shake them both awake. No time like the present, had always been his motto. No point waiting, putting off the pleasures of today until tomorrow.

His eyes, by now accustomed to the lack of light, feasted on his friends. The boy lay on his back, his arms above him on the pillow. The silver chain that always hung around his neck was barely visible, semi-buried in the shaggy chest. Bruno looking blissful in repose. The tightly muscled stomach slowly moving as the diaphragm expanded, the legs serenely parted, and between the thighs Max noted, for he wasn't slow to notice things, her shock of wild and ink-black hair. This is something new, he thought. Something rather interesting.

Her head, he thought. She's placed her head, face down, between his legs. No doubt to help her sleep. (She'd often said she used to suffer from insomnia. Her over-active brain, she used to add.)

At first he thought he might be dreaming, enduring some corrupt, tormenting vision in the dark. But then he caught a whiff of something female, something slightly fetid, in the air, and recognised that what he might have thought was just a putrid fantasy was happening: her face was in the newboy's lap.

(The groin-word gave him too much pain. He couldn't use it. Not just yet. That hard and shining nugget of reality had lodged, unswallowed, in his throat.)

He cast a second, furtive glance, and then he stared, then scrutinised. Her head, he almost said. Those legs, he could have added. Or thighs, to be exact. The lean and parted thighs, her low and sated breathing. The blithe, unknowing interaction of the quietly sleeping copulants. You two, he thought, you happy two.

He would have flopped back on the pillow, were there not the danger that the very act of flopping, the falling of his sagging form against the cushion, might have woken them. For now he focused all his strength on not disturbing them, on leaving them to rest in peace beside him.

The wine was re-fermenting in his gut, bubbling like a filthy witch's brew. He was desperate not to shake the bed, he didn't even want to tremble, or let some small, protesting sound escape his lips, in case they jerked awake and saw him. They'd peel themselves apart and see him all alone. And then they'd laugh, and he'd be finished. The best of him would shrivel up forever.

So he knew he had to keep quite still. Make sure he didn't make a noise. I might be silent, he told himself, but I'm screaming inside. Ironic use of cliché, he added. Make light of it, he summarised. Rise above it, if you can. It happens, now and then. Doesn't mean a thing. She must have done it in her sleep, like the unselfconscious slut she really is. Accept it, he advised himself. Try to be sophisticated. Pretend you've got some Gallic blood.

Carefully, he clambered from the bed, and felt the polished wooden floor against his naked feet. (He'd never been a carpet man. Matting from the Orient, perhaps, but never fitted carpets. His image didn't lend itself to signs of domesticity. Plushness wasn't really *him*.)

He padded softly across the room. Something pulsed inside his skull, and bile was rising in his throat. He reached the bathroom, stepped inside, and locked the door behind him. For he wasn't one of those who had a lockless bathroom. Not one of those degenerates who let their guests surprise them, as they squatted on the bowl. He might have been Bohemian, but he wasn't one for decadence.

He wanted them to comfort him, the pair of

them to hold him close. He'd been abandoned in his bed. The bastards didn't need him, any more. The reptiles didn't want him, and he ached with it, the sense of loss, the total isolation.

But nothing new, he thought, for he'd eaten, in his time, his share of faecal matter, he'd licked his heaped and fragrant dinner-plate of excrement. Developed quite a taste for it, in fact. And now they'd served him up another helping. Just to whet his appetite, and to show they really cared, they'd served him up a newly-minted, freshly-steaming turd. With garnish.

Flicking on the bathroom light, he crossed the floor and reached the basin. He gripped the sides, and bent his head, and thought of what he'd seen – the buried face, the parted thighs, the all-excluding happiness – and watched the brownish jet which issued from his mouth splash down into the marble bowl.

He felt better straight away. The cleansing nature of a decent spew, the healing effects of a good, hard puke, were often underestimated. Regurgitation, he remembered, was often quite uplifting. He peered, with modest admiration, at the steaming mess he'd made. Scraps of red and undigested pepper, which he vowed he'd never eat again, poked up at him through an otherwise bleakly uniform sludge. He bent a little lower, and sniffed a little deeper.

It stank, he realised, of vomit. How foul it was, how truly rank the smell, how deeply-felt his longing to rub foreign faces in it. He turned on both the taps, and let the water run, and washed it all away. He watched the peppers disappear. He watched them spiral down the hole. Goodbye, he thought. Farewell, my lovelies.

The mirrored cabinet above the sink, the single shelved and fitted unit in the bathroom, had been divided up a while ago. The lower shelf was his, the upper one was Bruno's. (She didn't have a shelf, of course, and he allowed himself to wonder, for a second, where she kept her things. He gave himself a moment's pause to ponder her arrangements.) The first-aid kit was at the back, behind the aftershave and talcum powder. Inside the metal box, and beneath the sterile bandages, was a pair of golden scissors, never used.

He found, to his disgust, that they were fairly poor in quality. He poked his thumb and finger through the holes. The hinge was loose, and he had to hold them gingerly, as he didn't want to stab himself, being of a type averse to pain.

He knew his hair would have to go, but cutting it, he recognised, would not be easy, indeed might even prove quite difficult. He began to chop away, though carefully, methodically, making sure he didn't stray too near the scalp. He left about a quarter-inch of tuft, or thereabouts, and when he finished gazed into the glass.

Not bad, he thought, but not quite there. Not quite the image he was seeking.

He filled the sink with lukewarm water, dipped his fingers in, and flicked away some drops. This was what he did the best. He'd always liked to lather-up. He spread the whitish cream around his head. It made him look angelic, like an ageing Shirley Temple, and he very nearly had to spew again.

He felt it better not to use the electric shaver. (The noise, he thought. The sleeping guests.) He took his ancient razor, an old-style, cut-throat razor, and drew it slowly through the foam. After every other sweep he dipped the razor in the sink and shook away the black-flecked cream. The act of transformation gave him unexpected pleasure, if not exactly ectasy. It pleasured him to shave his head, to hold the skin quite taut and scrape a razor-blade across it.

By the time he'd finished, by the time he'd sheared the top and sides right down to stubble, the foamy water had turned to grey. A film of hair-clogged lather floated on the surface. Scum, as he recalled, always rises to the surface. When he stared at the mirror, a stranger stared back, all jaw and jutting bone. That's me, he thought. That's really me. He looked, at last, like what he was. The inner man was mirrored in the outer form. So hard. So very different. Such sudden, vicious beauty.

Come and see me now, my friends. Pair of filthy whores, I'm ready for you now. Come and poke your scabby heads inside the door, and see me now.

His skin felt sore, and he gently touched the bristles on his scalp. When he took away his palm he saw a trace of blood, the barest, slightest, thinnest trace, but still a smear of blood. He washed his hands, and rinsed them clean. There was something in the soap. Some scratchiness embedded in the soap. He picked it up, and peered at it, and examined what he'd found. A piece of moulted houseguest. A strand of *arriviste*. A thread of pubic covering. A coarse and twisting Bruno-hair.

Call him priggish, if you will, but other people's sediments, their hidden seepings and damp effusions, he'd always found repulsive. Call him prudish, if you must, but spare him from the odours of his neighbours.

Nor was he more indulgent with himself.

Indeed, his own nocturnal emptyings, familiar though they were, he often found repellent. (It showed, he felt, consistency, at least.) But this Bruno-thing had gone too far. This Bruno-thing would have to be resolved. He'd overstayed, and now he had to leave. They'd reached their Bruno-threshold long ago.

He pressed his forehead up against the cool and mirrored glass. The bacillus would have to be removed, and then they'd settle down again. She'd love him once again. She'd save herself for him and be his woman, once again.

He knew she'd like the scalp. She'd appreciate the shaven scalp. He'd drape her on the floor, and spread her out, and rub his skull where she was tender. He'd let her have the pleasure of his rough and bristled scalp. His skin began to stretch and itch. He'd do it soon, he'd let her have it fairly soon, fuck the little fucker with his cranium.

He knew it would appeal to her. He knew it absolutely. He felt immense with knowledge, and almost strode into the room and did it straight away. He very nearly went back in, and laid her out, and gave the girl some trouble with his stubble.

Let the newboy watch and learn. Let him see a master at his craft. Let him see how someone civilised could do it.

He pulled the plug and emptied the bowl, then turned on the tap and let the water run. He wondered whether Bruno might have heard it. He wondered if the running water gurgled in his dream and made his innards tighten, if a spasm seized the famous Bruno-bladder and told it to evacuate.

Serve her right, he thought. Make her be a touch more careful, as to where she put her lips. Teach her not to roll and stretch between her boys, and let her mouth sag open in her sleep.

It would completely serve her right, he thought, and turned the tap on full, and let the water run.

15

'I'm going to take you out tonight, so you mustn't let me down,' he said. 'Not in front of other people. Not in public, so to speak.'

He had sat her on the bathroom stool, had gripped her in his knuckled fist and pushed her firmly down, and now he stood behind her, now he spread his hands and placed them on her skull. The barest touch, which barely made her quiver.

The voice was uninflected, completely self-controlled, a snake-like hiss that kissed her ear. He kept his precious store of venom bottled up inside. Secreted, should he need it, for some future confrontation. He didn't want to waste the bile, release it prematurely.

Knowing how he really was, his basic needs and inclinations, she derived a certain pleasure from the thuggish self-restraint. So when he touched her, when he ground his teeth and laid his hand upon her head and barely touched her with his fingertips, she felt the lightest tremor, the slightest tingle of excitement, the merest hint of damp delight.

'It's time to recognise reality,' he said. 'Take a look at what you are, a truly honest look. Be brutal with yourself, for once. Remember that the mirror never lies.'

He turned the foreign skull towards the glass.

'Not a pretty sight,' he said. 'A somewhat unexpected pallor for one who lives a life like yours, the hedonistic life of one whose every orifice is filled to overflowing.'

He stroked her hair. He played with it. He slid his fingers through the curls and took a generous portion, a permed and tinted chunk, and jerked it up, so that a slab of harsh, electric light fell on her face.

'Bright lights just aren't you, my love.'

He tilted his head and gazed at her reflection.

'You're more what one might term low wattage. Not a bright-light female, frankly.'

He peered, and leered, and softly jeered.

'It takes a special kind to bear the light. A youthful, nubile, luscious kind. You know the sort.'

He smiled at her.

'You must have seen them, once or twice.'

He pressed down on a brass catch, and a make-up box flipped open. He'd booked her in for a special session, an hour or two of private interaction. He'd sat her on the bathroom stool, pushed her firmly down, and now he stood behind her, big with rage, engorged with loathing, malevolence personified.

'I don't know why,' he said, 'but you don't exactly glow with joy. You don't exude a sense of sated satisfaction. In point of fact,' he said, 'you don't exude at all.'

She saw the mirror-image of herself. She couldn't help but see it, for he'd clamped her head and turned it to the glass. But when she saw it, when she saw the drained, anaemic image in the glass, she shut her eyes and pushed away the creeping recognition that those things they did, those rank and furtive things – the poking deep inside, the rubbing raw, the mess they made, the joys they gave – might bear a heavy price.

He stuck his hand beneath the lid and rummaged in the box. The sounds of wood and tortoiseshell colliding. He slid his thin and graceful hand inside the lacquered box. A man with such a hand could well have turned to music, might well have played the violin, or so he often felt. He knew his nails were beautiful.

He didn't bite or cut them, he always filed them down. (He'd bet she'd never known another man who buffed and filed his fingernails.) He loved his shaped and contoured nails: the crescent shape of cuticle, the classic paring of the ends, the constant grime beneath the rims.

A wealthy man with dirty nails. The rigid and defiling finger. He knew what girlies really liked.

'I think a touch of colour.'

He withdrew a small and oblong palette.

'One's heard it often helps.'

He flicked it open.

'Bruno says I've got artistic tendencies, but I think he's trying to wind me up. Implying something's not quite right.'

He selected a thick-stemmed brush.

'Making out I'm holding back. He often does that, actually. Between ourselves, that's what he does. Insinuates, I mean. Quietly undermines.'

He ground the stub into the powder, and brushed the dust across her cheek. Half an inch below the bone, he brushed the rouge across her cheek.

'Doesn't quite come out with it, just drops these vague remarks, these stinking, little hints, then sniggers with some slag we know . . .'

He dusted in the hollow.

'. . . some smirking, foreign slag.'

He narrowed his eyes and assessed the effect. Not bad, he thought. A glob of colour here, a sheen of powder there, and she'd be almost perfect, almost normal, very nearly what he wanted.

'Just because one might not always be entirely *ready*, doesn't mean one lacks the inclination. Tumescence being often overrated, as in time you'll understand. But I don't deny that there's a problem, and now I've had a chance to mull it over, to work out in my mind whose fault it is, I've concluded – on reflection – that it's yours.'

And then, with infinite care, and with total concentration, he drew the line around her lips, he made the shape he always sought and filled it thickly in. (The gloss, he promised, would be added later.)

He selected lilac for the eyes. Lilac on a purple background, if one's being accurate. Using thumb and middle finger to hold apart the lids, he applied a handsome smudge of kohl. Being what is known as kind, he warned her not to move while he was playing with the pencil. He told her not to breathe too much, impressed on her that she shouldn't squirm, nor move her lovely head. For eyes, as he explained, were very sensitive, and couldn't be replaced. Eyes should be for ever, he informed her.

Other substances were then applied, in no

particular order, and to no discernible plan. Tints and shades and iridescence. He painted out her foreignness, and made her far more neutral. De-Balkanised the little bitch.

Twenty minutes, and he was finished. A job well done, he told himself, and stepped back to admire his creation. He'd given her a pair of cupid lips, a beauty spot, two bright red circles on her cheeks.

'A fairly major transformation, if one might be so bold.'

He gripped her chin and turned her head from side to side.

'I think it's rather good,' he said. 'Don't you?'

She blinked at her reflection. She looked like someone else, like someone he'd once known, some hated vision from the past. Vermilion lips and scarlet cheeks. She looked obscene. She looked grotesque. She knew she ought to tell him, but would try to break it gently.

'Bruno might not like it.'

(Five simple words. Five simple, cutting words.)

'Fair point,' he said. 'That's very true. Bruno might not care for it. He's strange like that. He has his foibles, his little whims. He might not want you painted, might well prefer your natural state – some men like their women plain –

but a few cosmetic augmentations will never go amiss.'

He dipped his fingers deep inside an open jar, and moved his hand around, as if through mud, then brought it out, completely white.

'But then again, to quote yourself, the newboy might not care for it. He might not be amused. And we must consider *him*, we have to bear in mind our friend from Willesden Green, the ever-present newboy-factor.'

He placed his hand across her face.

'We call this cold cream,' he explained, 'in the liberal democracies. Because it's very cold,' he added, and watched, entranced, as her skin involuntarily twitched. He permitted himself a near-inaudible sigh of contentment, for he'd almost forgotten how very deep, how very profound, was his need to make her twitch.

He moved his creamy palm across her mouth, and she could smell the tobacco on his fingers. Smelly fingers and grimy nails. He knew his women through and through. He knew what girlies tend to like.

Spread wide out, his hand was large enough to cover her face. His hand was wide enough to blot her face right out. If he wished, if he only had the urge, he could have stopped her breathing, could have pressed the hand a little harder, ground the palm a little more decisively, completely blocked the nose and mouth. He could have done it, if he wanted. She acknowledged this, not unimpressed, as the white and freezing slime began to build between her lips.

'I'm glad you mentioned him,' he said. 'He'd slipped my mind, for once, so I'm rather grateful you reminded me of his existence, I'm really rather grateful, I really, truly am.'

He kept his cold-creamed hand around her face and came up close behind her. He pressed his coyly bulging groin against her neck.

'Mustn't forget the Bruno-boy. Wouldn't want to leave him out, disrupt our binary delights. I'd call that inexcusable, completely unforgivable, disgustingly self-centred.'

He rubbed his greasy palm across her cheeks. He spread himself all over, though careful, all the while, to cover every inch, each fractional expanse, of newly made-up skin.

'I'm doing this because I care,' he said, and slapped her once or twice, until she cried, then rubbed her face some more. He spread his cream from ear to ear, smoothed it round her nose, and tried to make it seep between her lips. He made her his anointed. He creamed the unprotesting countenance all over. He smeared himself across her face, and greased her till she shone.

'You're right,' he said. 'He might not be too keen.'

He gripped the oiled and shining jaw.

'Might not be quite his cup of tea, his glass of chilled and sparkling wine, to have you coloured-in like this.'

His fingers almost lost their grip, and he pressed a trifle harder. He didn't want to lose her. He didn't want to let her slip away.

'He might consider I've been presumptuous, might even think I've gone too far, might think it something of a liberty to paint my precious in his absence. Did that hurt? I'm sorry. It didn't hurt too much? I'm sorry. For these are brave and reckless times, and we've got to listen when he speaks, we've got to let him have his say. Minorities must always be consulted. The voiceless have to have a voice.'

When he took his hand away, she found the make-up had been smeared and spread, but not removed entirely. Tiny powder-warts had formed, and the colours had collided. She looked, she felt appalling.

'That's better,' he opined, 'by far.'

Bending down, he pressed his mouth against her ear. Such a delicate ear, so pink and fragile, so aching to be bitten.

'One hesitates to brag,' he murmured, 'but the house in which you sleep, the table where you feed yourself, the floor on which you often lie, the tub in which you're daily bathed, are mine.

'Possession is the core and crux of life, and you have to learn to love the one who keeps you. The upstart won't be here forever. A transitory type. Just passing through. He's here today, and gone tomorrow. Ephemeral, is what I'd call him. An inessential man.

'I've let him pitch his tent beneath my roof, because of my compassion, because a Bruno has to have a room, a corner he can call his own. And now the guest has settled in, and he doesn't want to leave. He doesn't want to go back home, he'd rather be with me. He'd rather tell himself he's put down roots with me. So here he is, and here he thinks he'll stay.

'And because I'm tender-hearted, because I've got what's called a tender, beating heart, I've let him, for a while. Just to pass the time. It makes a pleasant change, I thought, and it's only for the interim. A transient arrangement. It amuses me to humour him, and one does so like to be amused. As if you didn't know, you darling girl, you painted sow, you sweet, enticing piece of pus.'

He took the foreign lobe between his teeth, and prepared to chew, then let it go. He didn't want to damage it. He didn't want to spoil it prematurely.

'So don't forget,' he said, 'don't let it slip your mind, if you can possibly avoid it, that I'm the one, the single one, the only one who truly matters.'

16

When evening came, Max told the boy they ought to take her out to dinner. Let's take her walkies, as he put it, let's give the girl a breath of air. Because even dogs get taken out. Once they're trained, as he remarked. Once they've learned to love the leash. The little bitch would need her little bit of exercise, for her state of health was uppermost, it was always on his mind.

Bruno voiced a preference. He gave, as his opinion, that they might well try that place a minute down the road, that canal-side place with tables on the terrace. That was Bruno's input to the evening, his Bruno-contribution.

But Max declared they'd seen enough of rat-infested water. He said he'd rather show her something special, something rare and different that she hadn't seen before, something native to these islands that he knew she'd like.

Outside, in the street, they strolled towards the noise of Edgware Road. He'd had an urge to wrap a blindfold round her face, to keep her in the dark until they got there, but Bruno hadn't thought it wise. Bruno, with his lower-middle sense of what was right, had said some passer-by, some open-hearted element, some civic-minded wretch, would only intervene. So they strolled along and left her face uncovered. They let her see the sights of Maida Vale.

For a captivating instant, Max felt it all belonged to him. He listened as she oohed and aahed, and felt engorged with ownership. And then he watched her link her arm through Bruno's, and remembered where she liked to put her mouth, and realised that they made a charming couple. I must invite them home, he thought, and kept a pace or two behind, because he didn't want to crowd them, he didn't want to interrupt, he didn't want to feel himself intruding.

Droplets spattered on his head. The rain was spitting, more than pouring. It spat on him. It dampened down his hair and went inside his nose. It didn't seem to spit on them, but then, of course, it wouldn't. Bruno held her close. He kept her pressed up tight. Their heads were bent together, and they murmured indiscretions in the air.

Max kept a pace or two behind, and thought of what he'd done for them, that pair of graceless turds, those excremental ingrates. He'd given them a place to stay, he'd listened as they fumbled in the dark, then had to lie awake and sniff their odours when they'd finished, when at last they'd had their fill. And now they walked ahead of him, now they forged ahead of him oblivious and arm in arm.

Not fair, he screamed. Not fucking fair.

'We're here,' he said, and even smiled, his black-gloved hand compressed around the doorknob. They'd gone about a mile or so, spent thirty minutes strolling past the rubbish bags. The vileness of the area, its fetid lack of class. No wonder she'd enthused. Just right for her, he thought. Just up her street. Just up her dank and narrow alley.

The chip-shop reeked of fat, and oil, and ersatz friendliness. The server, with his peeled and shining face, glanced up but didn't smile. He merely glistened in the neon light, as if some friend of his, some caring pal, some muscled slab of live-in male companionship, had sat him down and spread that broad and moron face with cold-cream lubrication, from an open plastic jar.

Max felt the faintest mandarin distaste. He moved a fraction nearer to the counter.

'I don't know if you're quite aware of how you look,' he said. 'Or if it bothers you,' he added. 'The sweatiness, I mean, of your existence.'

He stared in awe and wonder at the bare and marbled arms, the broad and hairless hands which shovelled chipped potatoes.

'I only mention it,' he mused, 'in passing.'

The scraping of the metal trowel. That sound it made. That melody. He almost asked to borrow it, he almost asked the chip-shop man if he could take it, for an evening. He'd like to hold it in his fist, and shove it in, and have a scrape. Really get stuck in, he would. Clear her out completely. Get rid of all the muck, just scrape it all away. If there were justice on this earth, that's what he'd like to do.

He became aware of Bruno standing close beside him, Bruno softly mumbling, the Bruno-voice insistent in his ear. Bruno whining, whingeing, carping. Bruno always there.

'She wants to go,' the houseguest said.

'What's that?'

'She'd prefer it if we took her somewhere else.'

Bruno being good again. Considering her feelings. Bruno working rather hard at being rather British.

Max turned and gazed at her. He'd made her pure. He'd sanctified her crevices. He'd cleaned her very carefully. He'd scrubbed the tender skin until it glowed, because he cared, because he knew he'd take her out that night, and he wanted her to look her best. But did she give a damn for him? Did she give a moment's micturition? Did she use her painted lips to give him what she'd given Bruno? Did she? He was only asking.

She'd sat and let him wipe it off. She'd sat there, mute and passive, while he smoothed it all away, while he bent and fussed and worried, and he creamed it all away. She'd been watching as he worked, with her large, unblinking eyes. Hadn't made a sound. Just sat, and watched, and let herself be smoothed, she'd let herself be creamed, she'd let herself be gently wiped away.

(He must find out, it occurred to him, exactly where she came from. At least the country, if not the actual town.)

He would have gladly fed her chips, slid the cut and fried potato deep inside that sulky mouth. Salted, if she wanted. But always Bruno ruined things. She would have loved him, but for Bruno. Always Bruno. Always there.

The metal scraper scraped inside his head.

'So take her somewhere else,' he said. 'It's all the same to me.'

Max turned away, for he didn't want to see them leave. He didn't want to watch them linking arms and going off without him. He turned away, and heard the door bang shut, and nodded at the chipman's fingers.

'You ought to clean your nails,' he said. 'Just now and then. It makes a nice impression.'

The heaped and golden fish, which smelt not unlike cod, were spitting oil. They look quite good, he thought. Quite edible, in fact. And banana fritters wouldn't go amiss. Hot and wrapped and ready. Comfort food, for one who needed comforting. The very thought of it, the tantalising vision, put him in a state of oral expectation. He pointed at the oil.

'The heat of that,' he said, 'can reach as high as three hundred degrees. So you needn't wash the fish.'

The man behind the counter, who might well have been retarded, who might well have had deficiencies in mental application, shook his head to flick away the sweat above his eyes. Max watched in fascination. He liked to be at one with authenticity.

'It doesn't matter if you don't,' he explained, 'because the heat of the oil is more than sufficient.'

He raised his eyebrows significantly.

'The purifying heat of the oil. It burns off all the bacteria.'

The man was flicking fillets over, to do the other side. A single flick, and round they went. (Like Birthday Boy, the other day. Grasping foreign ankles with his grasping, newboy hands, and flicking round to do the other side.)

'So even though you never wash the fish, or clean the knife before you slice the potatoes – unless you buy them ready-cut, and I therefore stand corrected – and even if you let the sweat that's running down your nose drip off your chin and splatter in the batter' – he pulled out his wallet – 'the food's still clean.'

The man, whose pale and wispy hair was plastered down across his forehead, beneath his cardboard hat, wrapped a shovelful of chips inside three squares of paper, and passed the moist and pulpy bundle across the counter.

Max placed three coins in his open palm.

'I rather like you,' Max informed him. 'You're very good at listening.'

He unwrapped the paper and salted the chips, his hand pausing over the vinegar bottle before deciding to splash it on, to treat himself, regardless. For he doubted whether his tongue would get a chance to taste a better dish, that night. He had his doubts, it must be said, in the savoury department. But no matter. Let the other one, the self-abasing houseguest, be the one to crouch and lap. Let him take a golden shower, should he be inclined.

Outside it was cold and damp. He stood beneath the canvas awning, and fed himself with deep-fried chips. Now and then, though not too often, men in nylon anoraks filed past, trailing clouds of beer and sweat. He assumed they must have known he wasn't one of them, they must have guessed he was an altogether better type, an altogether different kind of customer. He stood and stuffed the prole-food in his mouth, and felt serenely satisfied, financially at ease, as he watched the lower orders filing past.

Only one thing marred the moment. Bruno and the girl. They'd gone, of course. They'd disappeared. They'd vanished without trace. Without a second glance. Without regret. Bruno and the girl. Bruno lapping with his greedy Bruno lips. He thought of them and had that taste once more, that taste that seeped up through his throat and filtered round his mouth. That bile-taste from the other night. He even might have spewed again, he might have brought up thick-cut chip and vinegar, had not the boy (whom he'd remember, ever after, and not without a certain fondness, as the chip-shop boy) appeared, as if from nowhere.

What brought the boy to Max, one couldn't tell. What made the stunted youth imagine he could cheek a Max, will always be a mystery. Perhaps it was the image Max presented, the reek of flaccid wealth that wafted round him, so that the boy could only see the fleshy waist, the turned up velvet collar, the unknown face of an unknown man, a man without an aura, standing hunched beneath the rain.

Whatever might have been the reason, the nameless boy passed by, and stopped, and doubled back. He stared at Max, and summed him up with adolescent eyes.

'Don't mind if I do,' he said, and reached inside the bag, plucked out a chip, and shoved it in his wet and grinning mouth.

An ugly, teenage face, Max thought, all bone and tufts and blemishes. A chainstore denim jacket, and full of upstart cockiness. He watched the boy go loping down the road. He watched him disappear, recede into the distance.

He compressed the greasy paper around the cooling chips and flicked it into the gutter. What a splendid piece of luck. How fortunate one often is. What bliss to be allowed to educate the younger generation. He licked the salt and fat and vinegar from his fingers, and rubbed away the residue, and pulled the leather gloves back on. He smiled into the dark and started walking down the road. He followed in the footsteps of the cocky, chainstore jacket.

A filthy Monday night, and all alone, abandoned by his guests, middle-aged and venomous and spat on by the rain, Max felt so grateful to the boy. He throbbed and ached with gratitude. He pulsed with rigid self-control, as he followed down the road.

You've done it now, he thought. You bastard prick, you thieving yob, you dropping from some vagrant's arse, you've really done it now, he thought.

You've made my night, my son.

17

He kept his distance from the boy. Thirty yards, or so. Not too close, to start with. There was no point getting intimate before they really had to. No point interacting, prematurely. He didn't want to frighten him, to make him bolt and run away, so he held himself in check, and he sucked his lower lip, and he kept a decent distance, just to start with.

The rain began to thicken. It hammered on his naked head and trickled down his neck, and every passing noise was muted. Even the sound his footsteps made was muffled, but somehow it excited him to hear it. He derived a modest pleasure from the slap of crafted sole against the pavement. And modest pleasures, as he'd come to understand, must be seized while they were there. Mustn't turn up snotty nose at slight and modest pleasures.

He watched the undernourished form – oblivious of what was yet to come, incapable of cosmic premonition – turn off the well-lit street and enter what, to Max's gleeful eye, appeared to be an alley-way. That's my boy, he thought, as he followed close behind. You're for it now, old mate. Mummy can't protect you now. And he felt the familiar warmth of something stirring down below, as if a hand were gently holding him. A hand that really cared. Perhaps his very own.

No one seemed to be about. All of them, all the namby-pamby wholesome types had stayed indoors that night. Only bits of low-life prowled the streets, scab-faced youths with their braggart pose and girlish lips, and those who came behind, those who followed close behind and felt they hadn't had their due from life. Slightly bitter men, who often answered to the name of Max.

A few yards further on, beneath a yellow lamp-post and beside an empty rubbish skip, the boy had stopped to light a cigarette. He cupped his hand around the weed and sucked in yellow smoke, as if his growth weren't stunted quite enough. Max stood there in his handmade suit and watched the unsuspecting boy. He watched him hunch his narrow shoulders, and cup the glowing tip against the wind.

Bruno smokes, he thought. Bruno sticks tobacco in his mouth and drags the smoke inside. And Bruno isn't stunted, more's the pity. Bruno isn't short of breath, Bruno doesn't wheeze. Bruno's lungs, like Bruno's other parts, would never rot or calcify. Bruno seemed immune from harm, chosen not to suffer.

Not fair, he screamed, and stepped a little closer.

'You took my chip,' he said. Or murmured rather, for he tended not to rant, if he could help it. He always did his utmost not to cause a scene. So he murmured, when he said his piece. He breathed the understated words, and watched the cloud of wordy breath condensing in the air.

The boy allowed his mouth to sag. The darkly shining hole began to grow. (Such curling lips, he had. So glistening with juices.)

'Sue me,' he replied. A slightly rasping, newly-broken voice, and the puny self-assurance of the young and brave and stupid.

Max listened to the voice, and saw the hairless chin, and felt the dam begin to burst. He felt a wave of something viscous bubble up inside, some densely misanthropic gel that boiled and foamed and pressed to be released. He heard the adolescent voice, and saw the crudely unformed face, and had an urge to spurt his precious bile across it.

I'm a thug, he thought, admiringly. I'm a nasty piece of work.

'Let me try to clarify.'

He'd try to put it simply, reduce the problem to its barest, and most pure, essentials. Elucidation, he decided, would clear the path to retribution.

'You shoved your hand,' he pointed out, 'the hand with which you pick your nose and wipe your rectal orifice – the hand which might, for all I know, be the one with which you ruminate – you shoved that hand inside my paper bag, and stole my chip.'

Max felt he'd put it rather well. A fair rendition, he told himself, a succinct summation, of what had just transpired. And phrased with a certain elegance, if he weren't too much mistaken.

But all wasted on the boy, of course. The young and scornful face, which maybe saw a razor once a fortnight, watched him closely, sized him up, and found him wanting. Recently pubescent, with gangling limbs and dangling you-know-whats, he wasn't too impressed by what he saw. For what was Max, to the casual eye, but a velvet-collared gentleman, a wine-imbibing liberal type who'd strayed too far from home?

'You want it back? I'll stick my fingers down my throat. You can have it back, if you want it back.'

Max sighed and shook his head. He felt reverse-paternal towards the boy. Anti-protective, to be precise. Destructive, in a word, was how he felt, and he'd always been a feeling kind of man.

'It's not the chip,' he said, 'as such.'

A non-committal shrug.

'It's the principle of the chip.'

The muscles in his neck went tight, the rain was drumming down again, and he felt a tension-headache coming on. This pestilential boy, this mucoid type, was deliberately upsetting him. He'd have to be persuaded to desist. He'd have to be encouraged to control himself.

'I don't know if I mentioned it, but I rather like your jeans.'

His skull began to ache, and he wished she hadn't left him. She should have been here when he wanted to perform, not vanished down the Edgware Road, not slipped her arm through newboy's and departed, not taken all her sediment and flounced off somewhere else, not left him all alone. Not fair, he screamed, not fucking fair.

'Do *you* like your jeans?'

The slowly comprehending boy, who was standing very still – and was not entirely lacking in intelligence – nodded once. A single nod would be sufficient, as he didn't want to aggravate.

'I thought you might,' Max said. 'I thought you'd like them, as they're yours. There goes a bright young lad, I thought, who knows a thing or two. He's wearing denim jeans, I thought. No corduroy for *him*, I thought. He only gets the best, I thought. And good luck to him, I thought, as I watched him wend his spindly way along the road.'

A sudden gust of frozen air scraped against his face, and he pulled the velvet collar up. He didn't want to get a chill, or expose himself to wind-borne germs. (Tuberculosis, he remembered, was spreading fast among the lumpen.) He pressed the collar against his cheek. He enjoyed the feeling against his skin, that velvet feeling of his velvet collar. It reminded him of what he most adored, all things soft and delicate. Spring buttercups. Her sweet, young self. His testicles.

'And then I thought – because I tend to think a lot – that I'm not too partial to the face. I like the denim jeans, but I'm wary of the face. One has one's doubts, one's reservations, *vis-à-vis* your countenance. A problem there, I told myself.'

The rain came pelting down.

'So we'll have to sort it out.'

It was thudding on his skull

'It's for the best.'

He smiled politely at the boy.

'My name's Max,' he said, 'and I'm going to break your nose.'

Whippet-fast, the boy was already moving to the side, but Max, despite his middle age and heaviness, despite his recent lack of exercise, darted forward, suddenly nimble on his feet. He lunged a half-length forward, stretched out a black-gloved hand, and grabbed the unappealing youth. (For although he was a wealthy man, a member of the rampant bourgeoisie, he knew you have to lunge a bit, he knew you have to dart and weave, if you want to dig your fingers in a chainstore denim jacket.)

'Relax,' he said. 'Be over in a jiffy.'

He jerked the boy towards him.

'Enjoy the moment, if you can . . .'

And he butted him, quite neatly, on his adolescent nose.

The bone cracked open instantly. Must have been a softness there, to split like that. A lack of moral fibre in the upper nasal area. He held the boy a moment longer, then let him drop, in case he gushed too much, in case the scarlet effervesced and soiled his richman's coat.

He wished the slut-bitch could have seen him. He wished she'd stayed around to see the glory of the act. She should have seen what he could do, once he knuckled down and did it. The heartless foreign cow, she would have clapped her hands and done a little dance, if she'd been standing, watching in the road. She would have truly loved it, would have gone down on her knees and worshipped at his temple, had she only had the decency to be there, had she not gone off and left him all alone.

The connoisseur of chips lay on his side, sobbing quietly on the pavement, his bleeding face pressed flat against the stone.

It occurred to Max – as insights often did – that all his stress had disappeared. The tension that had gripped his neck was gone, the threatened migraine quite forgotten in the fever of the moment. His every nerve-end seemed to tingle, and he felt as though he'd plugged into a power source, as if electric current were running through him, and he understood that certain things were even better than the very best he'd done to her. He'd just indulged himself, he realised, in a novel, and far safer, form of sex.

He bent towards the juvenile, and thought how young he looked, how completely vulnerable. He didn't want to lecture him, to let pomposity intrude, but felt a word or two, an honest admonition, might impress on him the error of his ways.

'Take-aways aren't good for you. Home-cooked meals are always best.'

Reaching down to rearrange the Brylcreemed hair, he caught the vaguest scent, the faintest whiff, of something lavatorial, an odour redolent of public tiles and porcelain. (Again he thought of girly: the loose and constant seepings, the hot and steaming emanations, the way she liked to ebb and flow. He thought of her quite frequently, these days.)

I've helped to mould the future generation, he told himself, which can't be bad. As he turned and walked away, he ran the film of what he'd done inside his head. He played it back inside his brain and heard again that whiplash sound, that brief, enticing sound of snapping bone.

The rain was pelting down. It came blowing in his face, inside his open mouth, and Max was running through the night, running grinning through the night.

The total, wild delirium of doing something bad for once. Beating up an underdog.

Smashing what offended him. The video inside his head. The sound of snapping bone.

I did that, he thought. I made him into that. Reduced the boy to that, he thought. I brought him down to that.

The rain inside his open mouth. The grinning in the night.

18

Although he found it heartening that even someone middle-aged could interact with juveniles, he came to understand that it hadn't been enough. He realised that he'd been too all-forgiving. He'd let the adolescent off too lightly. The brief and vivid link they'd forged was broken far too soon, and on reflection what he'd done appeared quite minimal.

His clean and upright Maxiness, his flabby, human decency, had held him back again. His sense of what was just and fair had caused the boot to hesitate, and he'd turned away and left him conscious on the ground. They'd had a pleasant evening's interlude, he'd shown some fatherly concern, but he could have been more rigorous, he could have used more emphasis, he could have thought of Bruno, while he butted.

The chip-shop boy had known, of course. He must have gauged the sort Max was, the sort who wouldn't lose control, who'd merely grip the denim cloth and tap him softly with his head. The sort whose gentleness would always let him down. The chip-shop boy would know all that, for the sub-types always understood, the masses always took advantage, the low-life knew how far to go.

So this was what he felt, as he ambled back through Maida Vale. Of such a nature were his thoughts, of such a kind his introspections, and he mulled them over in his brain, he raked them with his mental fork. He brooded, as it were.

When he brought the scene to mind, recalled the instant of release, there was something incomplete about it, something slightly lacking, something not quite there. He spooled the film inside his head. Slow-motion, till the moment came. Freeze-frame the image. Hold it, for a second. Allow oneself to savour it, to let the juices surge and flow, and then relax, rewind the tape, and let it run again.

But even so, it sickened him to think of it. It made him want to stick his fingers down his throat and puke with self-disgust. When he thought of what he'd done, when he heard the sound of bone on bone, remembered how restrained he'd been, how completely Little

Venice, the vomit-scented loathing started welling up inside, for it hadn't been enough, he hadn't done the boy enough, he hadn't given him enough.

And no one there to witness it. He'd had to do it by himself, his pleasures taken all alone. No one standing by his side to share the flawless memory. No one there to squeeze his hand and wish him all the best. Where were all his bosom pals, his scrotal chums and fellow pervs? Where the hell was Bruno, when he needed him?

For one delicious moment, for a single pregnant second, he imagined turning round and going back to where he'd left the young malingerer. He'd scrape him off the ground, and drag him home, and lay him, as a gift, before his guest.

'Have a look,' he'd say. 'Take a look at what I did.'

The voice would rise a notch or two. He'd hear it start to climb the scale.

'See the things I did, and all because of you.'

The shrillness of a Max enraged, the quasi-female pitch and whine, the sheer lactation of the sound. But Bruno wouldn't care. Bruno wouldn't be impressed. Max could spit and swear and scream at him, could slap the darkly newboy face and break the nasal bones of half of London's youth, and Bruno, being Bruno, wouldn't give a toss.

He was conscious, quite abruptly, of a need to talk it through. Not to brag, exactly, but to share the luscious moment, to let the sweet sensations be conveyed to those less fortunate. He almost felt inclined to step inside the nearest booth and call the late-night radio. He'd do his very best to make them understand what they had missed. He'd try to make them comprehend the rare and heady joy of butting someone smaller in the face.

Let them quietly take it in. Let them strain their voyeuristic ears and drool with brackish envy, for he'd done what they could only dream of doing.

By the time he reached the waterway, the rain had almost finished. Reluctant drops fell down at sixty-second intervals, and disappeared into the stone. Home, he thought, disgustedly. The wanderer returns.

The boats were bobbing on their moorings, the portholes glowing in the night. He paused beside a peeling hull, and would have looked inside, he would have had a modest peer, were there not the risk that someone might have seen him, some resident might find him staring in the dark. And as Max liked to do his lurkings unobserved, he turned and quickly glanced away. One day, no doubt, he'd get to look inside, but not quite yet. One day he'd press his leering face against the glass and frighten little babies, but sadly not quite yet.

All the same, the sight of portholes bare of curtains, and bargees living wholesome lives behind the clear, uncovered glass, was something that he found disturbing. Perhaps they half-believed that drifting on some urine-coloured water in a better part of London would protect them all from harm. Or maybe they'd been told that retards of a humanistic nature are quite often left alone. Whatever, here they were. Ensconced inside their floating homes, and glad to let their decencies be seen by passers-by.

He was tempted, as he sometimes was, to lob a gentle half-brick through an orange porthole, for like many of good breeding, he quietly longed to vandalise, to go out in the night and hear the sound of breaking glass. He knew he'd never dare, but they asked for it, to live like that. It shouldn't be allowed.

When he reached his house and went inside, he didn't go upstairs. He didn't wish to go to sleep. Not absolutely straight away. The crumpled sheets, the body smells, the sediment they might have left, their wordless self-absorption, were not entirely what he needed. Not at that moment. Not just then.

He opened up the cupboard in the hall. In here, he thought, is where it was. He rummaged on the shelf, and delved inside a cardboard box. In here was where he left it.

He shoved his hand right in, he scrabbled in the junk and tack, until he touched the metal can, and pulled it out, and turned it upside-down. It felt half full. Sufficient for his purposes. He wouldn't need too much. A half-full can would surely do.

He went outside, and found the rain had stopped completely, it didn't even spatter, it wasn't there at all. He idly shook the can and prepared himself to do the job. Been dragging on too long, he thought. Have to sort it, fairly soon. He'd have to bring things to a head, and resolve the pressing Bruno-problem. For as he'd come to realise – almost sadly, almost with regret – one could have too much of anyone. It was possible for newboys to overstay their welcome.

The rattle of the can, as he shook it once again. It was time to let the people speak, to put the writing on the wall. Even men of wit and grace can put graffiti on a wall.

The two-foot parapet, a slab of grubby stone, was crouching in the darkness. He squatted down, and chewed his lower lip, and tried to conjure up some pithy phrase, some slogan that would sum it up, some clear and unironic words with which to purge himself.

Once he'd clarified his thoughts, he kissed the metal aerosol, and pressed the button down. Liquid sprayed out from the nozzle, and he let himself inhale the fumes, he breathed in honest lungfuls of toxicity. He coughed, and laughed, and coughed again. Read this, you prick. Just feast your eyes . . .

He sprayed on to the wall. He spurted out his sentiments, and wrote them on the wall. But nothing too elaborate. Nothing too obscure. Just pressed his finger down and wrote his feelings on the wall, his 'BRUNO OUT!' conviction that he sprayed on to the wall.

When he finished, with a flourish, his thighs were quietly aching and his calves were softly throbbing with the strain. He squinted straight ahead and tried to read the words, but could barely make them out, could see them only faintly in the gloom. But even so, he swelled with pride, he bulged with manly self-approval when he realised that he'd written it himself, he'd done it all himself.

His last and final testament. His pure, uncoded message to humanity. He peered a little closer. It's really rather good, he thought. One's created something beautiful.

But dare one call it Art?

19

He didn't want to wake them, so he tiptoed up the stairs. He who butted passing louts, he who spurted on the wall, went padding up the stairs. In stockinged feet, on tippy-toes, he slithered up the stairs.

A siren sounded faintly in the distance. He reached the landing. Paused and listened. The police already on the hunt. (The well-built lads were always keen. They always liked to get their man.) For a second he indulged himself in damp, unspoken fantasies: they'd take him to the Scrubs, and then the horror would begin. They'd let festivities commence. He shuddered with enthralled dismay, for he knew he was the type that convicts interfered with.

The siren wailed. Coming nearer. Perhaps they'd found the splattered boy, and as he sobbed and whined and slurped the proffered tea, he told them they should seek a man called Max. Soon they'd come and get him. They'd come inside his home – all brawn and brute command – and drag him out, and throw him rudely in the van. They'd pin him to the metal floor, and then they'd grin and drive away. (The nauseating thought of being pinned by those who grinned.) It wasn't fair, he felt, that a man like him could get sent down for a boy like that.

But what they'd do to him. My God, he thought, the things they'd do. The rituals he'd undergo, the openings they'd have to search. The prodding and the poking. The squeezing and the choking. Being gripped by lesser breeds and forced to bend before them. (His sweet, unsullied sphincter moistened in advance.)

His mind was idly contemplating further, and more intimate, scenarios (choosing bunks and making friends, the daily slopping-out), when the siren passed below and disappeared. Relief washed over him, the mental burden was removed, and he scratched that fold of skin which always seemed to itch.

He realised that he loved himself. He frankly couldn't help it. The self-obsessed neurosis didn't worry him at all. That's me, he thought, that's Maxie-boy. Always anxious, always brooding. Not like others one could mention, who slept and drooled and trusted. Not like happy, boring types who felt they were at peace, newboy types who thought they'd found a home, who didn't like to plan too far ahead. The bliss, he thought, of living for the passing moment. The childlike bliss of being Bruno.

He stepped into the room, and peered towards the bed. Surprisingly, although asleep, they lay quite far apart, as though without his dumb and aching presence they no longer had the need to touch and lick and fondle quite so fervently. Quickly he undressed, and slipped between the sheets, wide-eyed and watchful in the dark. Traffic shadows moved across the ceiling, and he played his favourite video once more: the shop, the rain, the chip, the boy. The crack of brittle bone.

He thought about the night's events. He contemplated what he'd done, and what still lay ahead, and knew he'd chanced upon the simple truth that violation elevates. The urge to crush and desecrate was all that split the human from the pig, divided him from all that stank and wallowed in the mire. It was the single virtue that could raise him up, lift him high above the herd.

The girl would never understand. She, who bore it all with peasant fortitude, who knelt and chewed his cud with cow-like rumination, could never grasp so rarefied a concept. Not even if he sat her on the floor, and stuck a piece of plaster on her lips, and smoothed it down, and explained it, using short and simple words.

How could she, after all, with her longing to submit, ever comprehend what drove him? But she had her function, he admitted, her pre-ordained vocation. And when he thought of her, as he often did, he felt so kind and giving, so well-disposed towards her every slot and hidden crevice.

And then, as happened rather frequently of late, these thoughts he had, these sentimental yearnings of the spirit, led on to greater things, and a damp and formless longing sprang to mind.

Reaching out, he touched her in the dark. He knew he was a thug, a nasty piece of work, and he held himself respectfully and touched her in the dark.

20

I think it's time you went, old son. Time you packed your canvas bag and said goodbye.

Max played the words inside his head. He let them trickle through his brain. They sounded rather good, he felt. They had a certain *ring* to them. Tremendous words, they were. Two brief and cogent sentences, quite clear and unambiguous. No subtext, so to speak. No need for deconstruction.

It was a lazy, London afternoon, and she'd been bathed and tied and left indoors. The pair of them (the boys, that is) were sprawling on the terrace in the sun. The weather was unseasonally warm, and they'd lunched quite well, as usual, almost to the point of being bloated. They'd fed themselves with mild abandon (a fresh-tossed salad here, a char-grilled fillet there), and now felt stuffed with vitamins, a not unpleasant stretching of the gut, a sensual repletion of the spirit.

A dove had come to rest beside the railings, the mildest breeze was lapping all around, they were sipping cups of double-strength espresso, their little girl was gagged and keeping quiet, and it could have been a paradise on earth. It could have been so beautiful, had Max been more relaxed. But Max was facing problems of a fundamental nature. Problems which refused to go away. Specifically, the one he called the newboy-problem.

Reclining quite becomingly, Max rapped against his knee with a rolled-up magazine. He softly tapped the bone. He gently beat himself in time to some secret, mental tune. He sat beside his newboy-friend and thought the problem through. Gave it his complete attention. Cogitated manfully.

The revulsion that he felt, when he contemplated Bruno, had been something he'd repressed, at first. It seemed somehow too beneath him, too vaguely infra dig., that a man like him should need to hate a man like that, as if by hating Bruno he debased himself. For what was Bruno, after all, but one who'd climbed above his natural place, one who'd crawled out from his mother's hole, and rinsed off all her slime, and taught himself to play the game, and now stood, darkly panting, by the bed?

And that side of things, that scummy side, was daily getting worse, for what Bruno lacked in viciousness, he made up for in lubriciousness. It sometimes seemed as though whichever end the newboy took, whatever role he chose to play, however limbs were bent and spread, he always got the best of her. He always seemed to know how far to go. He had a greediness to pleasure her, as if her pleasure even mattered, and she, the fickle, foreign ingrate that she was, would arch and sigh and let herself be moved to sullen ecstasy.

So Max rebuked himself, at first. He took himself to task, in a non-judgmental way, for finding Bruno guilty of being what he was. Ungenerous thoughts, he told himself, had never been his vice. He'd never been the type to cast a stone. Malevolence was foreign to his nature. Yet here he was, an upright man, seized with choking detestation. It surely meant the newboy was to blame. To evoke such pure and undiluted loathing, he'd have to be to blame.

He felt much better once he realised that his attitudes could only be expected. There was nothing wrong with him at all, for Bruno-hatred was organic, a precious bloom that he could nurture in the dark. So he forgave himself, absolved himself from guilt, and often rocked himself to sleep by counting Bruno's sins.

But even so, the blitheness of the boy began to grate, the sheer complacency began to get him down. The handsome face, that sneering mouth, the ease with which he made her happy. The contentment that he daily oozed was more than Max could take. Yet what, perhaps, intrigued him most was that the cultivated Bruno, the Bruno who behaved like he belonged, was just as jarring, in his jarring way, as the hidden, shrieking Bruno, the glob of protozoic slime which lay beneath the surface.

Max sighed and squinted at the water. He knew he had the grace to shy from confrontation. Nobility would always hold him back. Not for him to cause a scene, to scream and shout and make demands, but there came a time when one just had to make a stand, although the phrasing of it troubled him. Perhaps he'd try to put it more obliquely, endeavour to surprise the boy, catch the houseguest unawares. He'd sidle up and whisper something subtle in his ear. Or perhaps he'd better blurt it out, come spurting loudly from the mouth. He mulled it over in his head, and settled for a modest blurt. A short and pithy verbal spurt.

'I'm afraid you'll have to go,' he said.

'I think I'd rather stay.'

'I'm sure that's very true. But all the same,' he said, 'it's really time you went. Time to bugger off, old bean.'

Bruno took this statement in. He felt it resonate inside his head, and penetrate his brain, and slowly sink into his consciousness. It seemed so typical of Max to want to spoil it all, to try to prick the perfect bubble of his bedmate's peace of mind.

He leaned back in the wicker chair and scratched his upper thigh until the skin turned almost pink, then spread his muscled legs and rearranged his boxer shorts. (The latter so that air might freely circulate, and fragrant breezes would caress the famous Bruno groin.)

Max couldn't help but notice, he couldn't help but let his vision hover, for a second: the leaning back, the spreading out, the muscling of the muscled legs. It meant nothing if he noticed, for he was only mildly curious. But he glanced away in time, he made sure he flicked his eyes away, in case it might be thought he'd stared too long. For it wouldn't do, it frankly wouldn't be good form, to let his drooping gaze be seen to linger on that special place, that dark and reeking Bruno-place she'd made her very own.

'I like it here,' the newboy said.

It seemed somehow quite perverse, almost verging on the odious, that he should have to leave. For surely he had done his bit, he'd made his contribution to the welfare of their little group, and ought to have the right to stay a while, to have his share of goodies, while they lasted?

'I've settled in,' he added, draining bitter liquid from his cup in one audacious sip. 'I've put down roots.'

Max lit a small cigar. Reflected sunlight speared and probed inside his head. It made his eyes begin to burn, and his skull begin to ache.

'We'll have to do some weeding, then.'

He sat and smoked and brooded. His world, the world they'd given him at birth, the one bequeathed to him, the one they'd said was his by right, was slowly being eaten up, and what remained imploded while he sat and watched. Everything was dirt and grime. He knew it wasn't him. Those filthy things they did to her weren't really him at all. Bruno led him on. Bruno, with his undiminished appetites, had instigated everything.

And now the boy was being difficult. Now he'd start to whinge and whine, and try to play for time. Max sucked in smoke and glanced across the water. A woman opposite, dressed in pink and black, was parading on her balcony. She must be new, he thought. She's just moved in, he told himself. Some *nouveau* type, some fat and preening parvenu, to be avoided.

He shaded his eyes and peered at her: clinging, tight-cut leggings, and a scooped and shiny top. To his cool, disdainful eye she looked quite appallingly common. The breasts, in particular, he found unfortunate. Huge and hard, as if they were synthetic, as if some god-like surgeon had sculpted them, one afternoon, for a fairly handsome fee.

If he recalled correctly, if he weren't too much mistaken, he'd never been enamoured of the breast. He'd never felt too partial to the titty. Mammaries had always left him cold.

Bottoms, need one say, were something else entirely. He wouldn't care to pass one by on a cold and rainy day. For like many from the upper ranks, like many with a private education, he was always ready to oblige, he'd do his unassuming best, for some pert and waiting buttocks.

So botties yes, Max recognised, but titties, sadly, no.

Suddenly it came to him how truly dreadful it would be, were the sac implanted in her chest to start to decompose, and the silicone were to leak away, and the gap it left began to rot, and the toxic mess began to spread . . .

Not nice, he told himself, and stopped that

train of thought. He pulled his mental emergency cord, and brought it shuddering to a halt. He brought it juddering to a stop, and realised, with an urgent rush of self-esteem, how disturbing was the image, how deeply it distressed him, how moved he was by suffering. He sat there, with his small cigar, quite awed before his own humanity, and remembered that he loved himself. Profoundly so, in fact.

'One's never really been a *bosom* man,' he murmured, and let his idle gaze seek out something more appealing.

Above the roof-line of the mansions opposite, rearing starkly up behind, was a thick and slab-grey rank of council blocks. So high, they were, so multistorey, they almost pierced the scattered clouds. He narrowed his eyes, and squinted into the light. Without pretending to be absolutely certain, he could have sworn that there were people staring down at him, their pale and vulgar facial blobs pressed hard against the window-panes.

It was a lazy, London afternoon, and he was sitting on his balcony, the way a free man should, and when he searched for meaning in his life, when he searched for what was true and lifted up his gaze to heaven, he found the underclass, to his disgust, was quietly gazing back.

'You've got to go,' he said.

'I don't see why.'

'Because I want you to.'

Bruno rubbed the stubble of his always-stubbled chin.

'She's used to being satisfied. I doubt that she could bear it, if I left.'

What a lad, Max thought. A very lippy, rather cocky, rash and reckless lad. He tilted back his chair, and grinned at the bleached-out sky.

'If you don't disappear,' he said softly, 'I'll make you disappear.'

'Fighting talk, old mate.'

'Believe me, Mister Minsker.'

'I like it when you say my name.'

'Do you?'

'I like it when you wrap your bloodless lips around my name.'

'Always sneering, always needling . . .'

'Someone has to.'

Max turned to face the younger man. He'd miss him, all the same. He'd miss the pouting mouth, those sweetly rancid odours, that torso with its mat of hair. He knew he'd miss his Bruno-boy.

'I've had enough,' Max said. 'A clever chap like you should have the sense to see it. The writing's on the wall, my friend.'

'But if I went, she'd sulk and pine.'

'I'm sure she'd cope. She's from the Balkans, after all.'

'I haven't got the heart for it. I couldn't deny her *me*.'

'I'll try to make it up to her.'

The houseguest shook his head.

'Some things, you'll find, just can't be faked.'

Max spread his lips. A flash of teeth. A brief, convincing grin.

'I'll miss you, Bruno.'

'I've not gone yet.'

'But when you do, I'm going to miss you.'

Max, who always felt so deeply, felt a kind of premature nostalgia for the Bruno days. They'd had their moments, after all. They'd had their times of share and share alike. But Bruno over-stayed. They always overstayed their welcome. He felt an urge to explicate, a need to make him understand.

'There's such a thing,' he said, 'as knowing when you're surplus to requirements. I let you step inside my home – a man I barely knew, and hardly liked – impose yourself upon my life, consume my food, imbibe my wine, and fuck, to call a spade a spade, my girl.'

'Our girl, old son. She's not a chattel.'

'She's mine,' Max said, and listened to his voice. He heard it start to climb the scale.

'That's what somehow quite escapes the

Brunos of this world. Those types like you, existing by the great goodwill of types like me. One doesn't want to be a bore, but you're frankly only tolerated, and sometimes, being foolish, you forget it.

'I found it rather droll, at first, to have you taking part, and I thought I'd let you stay. But you've overstepped the mark. You've gone too far. You've tried to push that bit you love, your favourite bit, that bit they clipped when you were small, a touch too deep.'

Such cruel and unkind words, they were. Such verbal laceration. Bruno trembled, very slightly. His mutilated member quivered with dismay. When he glanced across the water, he noticed that the woman who'd been watching them had gone. She must have disappeared a while ago, gathered up her pendula and taken them inside. Wonder who she is, he thought, as a discreetly modest ripple, a shudder that was barely there at all, spread along the surface of his skin.

Max, he felt, could be so graphic, so point-lessly explicit. And now he'd raised the subject that quite naturally enthralled them both, the huge, unanswered question of the massive Bruno manhood.

But both are well aware that it's not his piece of throbbing flesh that makes her so adoring, but the man behind it, the wielder of the blue-veined weapon, the one who makes her feel alive, who kisses all her bruises, before he bruises her again. Wherever she was moister, he'd be there. And always ready, always able, always willing, ever welcome. Even when they tossed for ends, he always seemed to win.

And she, the missing link, the squabbled-over object of their softly trickling desire, she never even knew. She would have been so touched, were she only conscious of it. Had she only sat beside them, had she heard her precious boys, she would have felt so proud. It would have been a kind of affirmation, had they had the grace to let her know. But each of them, in his separate way, was completely self-regarding. Each only wished to stroke himself, to suck and lick and fumble with his sweat-encrusted ego.

The sun had disappeared behind a cloud, and Bruno stood and stretched and yawned.

'I'm going in, if that's all right with you.'

He turned towards his host.

'It *is* all right with you, I take it? Because if it's not all right, if it's not entirely what I'd call all *right*, I'd be quite mortified.' A careful smoothing down of boxer shorts. 'I truly would.'

The drawing-room seemed cool and dark, by contrast with the terrace. A muted sound came wafting down the hall. A soft, endearing whimper of self-pity. They strolled along the corridor, and stepped inside the bathroom, and there she was, quite helpless on the floor. The bound and waiting immigrant was huddled on the floor. The saviour of their sanity, the polished marble floor.

'Seems close in here,' Max said.

Unchivalrous, perhaps, but it couldn't be denied. She was giving off such pungent whiffs, such tartly female odours. And that smear of red around her wrists. Max must have tied the cords too tight, and they'd rubbed the skin and made it bleed. (Though not too much, of course. With her, the flow was never too extreme. Excessively she never bled.) But all the same, they found that when they sniffed, they smelled the slightly heady scent of sweat and fear.

'Do you think she's had enough?' Bruno, with a sliver of concern.

Max considered for a moment.

'Probably,' he said. 'But surely that's the object of the exercise?'

'I take your point,' the newboy said. 'She always asks for more. She does keep coming back.'

'She does.'

'She's a glutton for punishment.'

'She is.'

They smiled in perfect understanding, for it

was at moments such as these – sublime, exquisite moments – that they felt as close as brothers.
Transcendent moments, when they stood and
watched her writhe and moan, and complicity
would bind them tight, and her breath became
quite laboured, and Bruno often sighed and
then, with mild alarm, would say:

'Do you think she's dying?'

And Max would fondly tilt his head and gaze
at her, their gently drooping flower, and say:

'Quite possibly.'

At times like these they almost banished from
their minds, if such were ever possible, their
uncontrolled antipathy. For she had made them
what they were. (She wasn't like the other girls.
Not a normal type at all, and abnorms ought to
stick together.) Then one of them would bend,
and touch, and stroke the velvet skin until she
shook, and Bruno, with his self-deluding sentiment, his civilised pretensions, would pull the
knot apart, and sit her up, and rub her with a
freshly-laundered towel, until the paleness disappeared, and the blue gave way to pink, and
she'd smile at him, and sometimes, being grateful, would kiss him where he liked it best.

But not that afternoon. That afternoon, she
merely let him bring the circulation back, and
touched his head in thanks, and slipped, unfet-
tered, from the room. She left behind a yellow

pool. Her moisture, on the floor. The host decided, just this once, that he wouldn't make her clean it up. Magnanimous, he let her go.

Bruno leaned his frame against the door. A man who looked at ease, Max thought. Provocatively at peace. Basking in contentment. Almost hog-like, he concluded. Almost wallowing. He had a sudden, sleekly hideous, intuition.

'I think you think you're better than me.'

Bruno moved his shoulders. A tiny, modest gesture of consent. Parodically, he shrugged. He didn't even try to look embarrassed.

'Not better, Max. Just quicker, brighter, stronger and younger.'

A brilliant, Bruno smile.

'And by the way,' he added, tearing off a length of sage-green tissue, 'been wondering where you find your pleasures, now you've got to seek them out, now that girly's getting choosy. Been wondering how you're satisfied, if, by chance, you take my drift.'

Kneeling down, he began to sponge the golden juice.

'Never quite got round to asking, what with this and that . . .'

Making circles on the floor, he soaked up all her mess. He spread the paper on the tiles and wiped away her residue.

'One gets by,' Max said. 'One manages.'

Bruno quietly grunted as he worked, for he liked to do his bit, he liked to get stuck in, he liked to have a natter with his friends.

'I suppose you tend to masturbate . . . ?'

Max spread his lips, and bared his teeth, and recalled the sound of snapping bone.

'I prefer to sublimate.'

Bruno nodded as he wiped.

'That's the spirit.'

He flicked a ball of sodden tissue into the porcelain bowl.

'Keep the old pecker up.'

Max tried to keep his face impassive. It proved difficult, but possible. There might have been a sudden shrillness in his skull, a single, sharp, stiletto hole inside his lung, a pool of vomit-panic in his gut, a ripping of the spleen, a sense of being caught on film, impaled on Bruno's tinted lens, but he kept his face impassive.

'One does one's best.'

'I know you do. And don't think I don't admire you for it.'

Bruno pulled the chain, then rinsed his hands and dried them on the nearest towel. The vigour of the rubbing of the towel on the skin. The energy of newboys when they're being energetic.

'You've got my total sympathy.'

'You ache for me . . .'

'I do. My every pile is bleeding with compassion.'

'It's such a shame you've got to go.'

'I know it is, but there you are.'

He let the towel drop.

'I'll have to wrench myself away. It'll break her evil heart, but can't be helped.'

'I sometimes think you've let yourself be taken in,' Max said, 'seduced by all those things she does.'

'Which things, in particular?'

'Specifically the other night. Specifically to you.'

Bruno saw the light.

'Ah,' he said. 'You mean *those* things.'

Now he understood, he got the gist of what was meant: the mouthiness of she who liked to leave her sediment on marble floors, the oral openness of absent friends, the unforced lippiness of those from overseas.

'No doubt you found it rather alienating.'

'Not at all,' Max said. 'I found it rather amusing, actually.'

'I thought you might have. I did hear you in the bathroom, stifling gleeful sniggers, if I'm not too much mistaken. And if I am, forgive me. Max is having fun, I thought. He finds it rather droll. Max is feeling quite amused. He's in the bathroom chuckling to himself, I thought, as I let her have her head, and she did specific things in a quite specific way.'

'So you weren't asleep.'

'Apparently not.'

'And her?'

This Max had to know. For it would have been unbearable if she had also heard him in the night, if she'd raised her generous head and heard him retching in the sink. The bitch, he thought, the lousy bitch, the lousy little buttock-spreading luscious foreign bitch.

'Was she also listening, then?'

Bruno put his hands behind his head and locked the fingers tight. For once he didn't pull the joints and click the bones. He managed to refrain from making finger-noises. Max was feeling stressed enough, he felt.

'I'm happy to report,' he said, 'she slept right through. Didn't hear a thing,' he added. 'Took a while, of course. You know the way she frets.'

Pause for brief, ironic smile.

'But once she'd shut her eyes, once baby had the dummy in her mouth, she settled down and drifted off to sleep.'

(Bruno seemed completely unaware, completely confident that nothing bad could ever touch him. He hadn't understood that things were different now, that life was unpredictable and Brunos were inflammable.)

Max tried to gather up his thoughts, but they sifted through his fingers, they slithered through his hands before he'd even grasped them. But simple concepts could be managed. Basic truths were evident. Bruno heard it all, the other night. With his overwhelming sense of being chosen, with his pity for the reject, with his deeply-felt compassion, he had lain there, in her mouth, and heard him spew.

And now the boy was standing, quite at ease, and trying not to smirk too much. Solidifying, doubtless getting harder by the minute, getting firmer by the second, while Max felt all his maleness disappear, he felt that all he valued in this life began to loosen, weaken, leak away.

Be female soon, he thought. Become a girly, fairly soon. I'll be like her, and suppurate, and have to wear a cotton pad, and bend before my betters.

He leaned a half-foot forward, speaking very softly, in his best patrician murmur, so that Bruno had to strain his ears, he had to stretch his aural faculties, to hear him.

'I think you're forgetting the point,' Max said. 'I think you're forgetting the salient point.'

'Do tell . . .'

'We're meant to synchronise. What we do,

we're meant to do together, and when she gives herself she does so, if I'm not too much mistaken, to us both.'

'I follow you entirely,' Bruno soothed, 'I'm on your side completely, but certain things just can't take place. They frankly can't be done.'

He tried to put it at its simplest, to avoid misunderstanding. No place for ambiguity, he thought. Better give it to him straight. Let him have it stripped of all adornment. Just tell it like it is, but try to put it nicely . . .

'She cannot suck us both at once. Not simultaneously,' he clarified, should clarity be needed. 'Now and then she gets the chance to choose. We give the slave a vote and let her choose whose cock she wants to suck. Happens all the time, old mate. I believe it's called democracy. And now she's in the West, now she's almost settled in the free and liberal West, it's time she learned our little ways.

'In short, she cannot do us both at once. I'm sure that if she could, she would, but I'm afraid she can't. It's just not feasible. Just can't be done, old son.'

On which conclusive note the houseguest paused for breath, and Max allowed himself a vision of enchantment, an enticing recollection of a puboid face, the smell of bulk-bought grease, the groundless self-assurance, the way

200

he'd folded as he fell. The bone-on-bone delight of teaching little runts they shouldn't loiter in the dark.

He ran the uncut tape inside his head, and revelled in the memory, the bleak, beguiling memory of a newly-gelded man.

21

'This is Sam,' Max said. 'He's come for tea.'

The open door revealed a little boy, a blond-haired child, a grave-faced infant with unblinking eyes.

'She won't be coming down today. Not foreign thing upstairs, I mean. Not she who leaks so shamelessly.'

He pulled the door still wider.

'Just thought I'd better mention it, in case you might be wondering.'

Bruno, standing on the porch, light-headed and mildly nauseous from waking up too early, expected more curvaceous sights than this. This was not a reason to have come. If this were all there were, he could have stayed in Rome and cut another deal. He could have pulled the sheets above his head, and kept the world at bay. He could have let the plane depart without him.

The bastard might have phoned to let him know. He might have warned him not to bother. Bruno could have stayed in bed and dreamed of her. Allowed his semi-conscious mind to do those things that even he, welcome as he was, had not yet plucked up courage to suggest. Instead of which, instead of stroking what he valued in his sleep, he'd rushed back from abroad, and climbed into his car, and driven through the rain, and now stood quietly dwindling on the porch.

'My little lad,' Max pointed out. (The pride of ownership, the relieved delight, the knowledge that he'd done it all himself.)

'Did you know I had a son?'

Bruno, shivering as he stepped inside, began unbuttoning his coat. His bones felt damp, as if the rain had seeped beneath his skin. Too cold outside, these days, and it seemed she wouldn't be around to warm him up. But what was Maxie asking him? Did he know he had a son?

'I didn't even know you had a sperm count.'

He shrugged off the coat and handed it over.

'But congratulations, all the same.'

He slid a thin cigarette between his teeth, winked at the boy, and flicked a gas-filled lighter with his thumb.

'Nice one, Max.'

He blew an almost perfect smoke-ring high up in the air.

'Must have done it right, for once.'

And then they laughed, the pair of them. The laddish lads, chock-full of scrotal fluid, knew how to share a joke. They never took offence, whatever might be said. It was merely part of all the usual banter, the short and curly phrases that they liked to fling about, testicular dimensions being measured, all the while. It helped them bond, to laugh life that. To stick these verbal spikes inside each other's tender parts, and have a gentle poke around, then neatly pull them out again.

'Shall we go through?'

Max showed the way, he led them down the corridor. His son, the small and budding male, the flower yet to bloom. And Bruno, with his Bruno-inclinations, his friend and fellow fornicant.

'My sister takes care of him, actually . . .'

'Does she really? How very nice of her. How very sisterly. Not just a son, it seems, but a sibling too. I turn my back, I'm barely gone a week, and suddenly there's three of you. Tremendous news. A trinity, no less.'

Bruno tried to picture her, he tried to conjure up the kind of woman that she was. The kind who'd sacrifice herself, devote herself to caring for her brother's salty mess, nurture what he'd squirted out one hot and reckless night. He tried to bring to mind some self-denying, stomach-heaving, soft and yielding image, but it proved elusive.

All he saw inside his head was Max in satin underwear, Max decked out in frills and bows, and blessed with generous mammaries, from one of which, cupped between his bony hands, emerged a thread of fresh lactation.

He pondered on the implications. He endeavoured to discern some buried meaning, some hidden truth behind this vision of a milk-producing Max. For with every single day that passed, he found he had a slightly more disturbing fantasy, a slightly damper deviation from a norm that was already somewhat deviant. But then, so much of it was new to him. So much was revelation, for a wide-eyed Ashkenaz from Willesden Green.

That Max could procreate was frankly quite commendable. Well done, old son. Full marks, old mate. And the sister sounded interesting. She might be worth an evening out. (A theatre trip. A cabaret. A dinner-date, perhaps.)

'Would I like to meet her,' he ventured, 'or would she remind me of you?'

'You're not her type.'

Max sounded particularly certain, for once. Dogmatic, almost, in the way he that he put it.

'You're sure of that?'

'I'm afraid I am. She wouldn't really *take* to you.'

'Is that a fact?'

'Alas, it is.'

But Bruno wouldn't let it lie. Bruno felt he had to know.

'Some special reason?' he enquired. Quite casually, and *en passant*, but he knew persistence often paid.

Max allowed the corners of his mouth to twitch. The slightest puckering of the skin, the barest movement of the lips.

'Afraid she lacks my liberal values.'

A suspicion of a smirk, though nothing more.

'She's what is known as unenlightened.'

It seemed a shame to have to give such unappealing news, to have to disappoint his phallocentric friend. But there you go, Max told himself. Such is life.

The boy was running on ahead. The plump and shining infant legs went pumping on ahead. He was steaming down the corridor, chuckling at some private joke.

'His mother goes to see him once a month.'

'That's big of her. My goodness, yes.'

Bruno sucked a little deeper on the weed. He

inhaled the scented smoke until it filled his lungs completely.

'We prefer if like that,' Max explained.

The fumes were hanging thickly all around, and he found he had to turn his head away, he had to re-locate his nostrils to avoid the Bruno-air. He detested other people's exhalations nearly as much as he loathed their secretions, and their secretions he loathed absolutely.

'The judge said she lacks maternal feelings. That's why I was awarded custody.'

Although the kitchen was unwelcoming, facing north and dull with winter light, the breakfast-table was a treat: heaped with different kinds of cake and jam, and wholemeal bread and cheeses for sophisticates. They watched the toddler, the golden-haired child, progress towards the casement window. Bruno felt, if not perturbed, at least a vague unease. Disclosures of an unexpected nature had never much appealed to him, and this latest one, potent as it was, he found especially unwelcome.

That Max could reproduce himself seemed somehow not quite credible, as if it contradicted all he claimed to be. That his ejaculations had some consequence, some meaning that extended further than the ceiling, was all too much to contemplate.

And a boy to boot, he told himself. A little lad

with all the bits he'd ever need to live a decent life. Produced by Max. Made in Little Venice. He found it inconceivable. Almost unbelievable.

Max had spurted out some creaminess, he'd done the famous deed and here it was, the living proof. Preposterous though it might seem he'd made a tiny blob of grinning immortality, and Bruno couldn't help but feel the slightest pang, the merest twinge, of envy.

'You got custody because she's a slag,' he said. 'That's what custody means,' he explained, and flicked away a drooping turd of ash. 'It means you married a slag.'

He scratched his jaw, pulled back his sculpted lips, and bared his pure white teeth. Such a man, he was. So beautiful. So clichéd all his attributes to those who didn't share them.

They let the slag-word hover, for a moment. They watched it as it hovered in the air, then floated down and settled on the polished wooden table.

'He looks good, though,' Bruno added. 'I'll grant you that. I'll grant you that he looks quite good.'

He watched the boy devour a slice of chocolate cake. Spawned by Max, he thought. Remarkable.

'Cherubic, almost.'

He stared a little harder.

'Not a great *resemblance*, though . . .'

'Isn't there?'

'No.'

'I can't say that I've noticed.'

'I know you haven't. There's a man, I've often thought, who doesn't notice things. Perception isn't what I'd call your forte. So take my word, old mate. He's not too much like Daddy.'

He took another, longer drag.

'Maybe if one didn't stand right next to him, and the light were fairly poor, and one were feeling fairly generous, he might, perhaps, resemble you. There might be early signs of similarity – a hint of bodily corruption, the promise of decay. If one didn't look too hard, there might be intimations of the way he'll finish up. What doctors no doubt term incipient signs of Maxiness.'

Complacent smoke came curling from his nose.

'But frankly, if one came up close and peered at him, and were to prod and probe that peachy flesh around his face, I doubt that one would find a smaller version of yourself.'

He poured himself a glass of lemonade.

'Though I might be wrong, of course.'

Max slid an ashtray past the heaped-up plate of cooling scones.

'He takes after her,' he stated. 'Like his mother,' he added, and heard his self-excusing voice, and nearly gagged. The lameness of the sentiment. The bleating sound he made. The sudden vision of that thing he had, that withered thing between his legs.

Bruno nodded in agreement, grinding out the stub.

'I dare say you're right.'

He leaned against the wall, released a final, blue-grey puff of smoke, and watched it slowly fill the room.

'Makes one think, though.'

'Does it?'

'Now you come to mention it, now you've tried to pin me down, I'd say it does. What it does is make one think. It makes one start to speculate. It makes one wonder if he's yours.'

With which humane remark he glanced towards the placid child, and found him eating guava fruit, intent and self-absorbed.

'You ever wonder if she hasn't fobbed you off with someone else's?'

The newboy had the grace to shrug, for he didn't want to caused offence. He didn't want to rock the boat, unless completely unavoidable.

'I'm only asking,' he excused himself.

Max couldn't bear the flat north light. He had to have the sun, to feel the sunlight on his skin, or he was finished. He had to feel some natural warmth. To comfort him, if nothing else.

Because she might have fobbed him off, she might have spread herself for someone else, allowed a better man to tunnel deep inside.

It frightened him to think of it, but what frightened him still more was loss of self-control, and now he felt it split apart. The face collapsed, the skin began to sag, the flesh beneath it peeled away. The waxy mask he wore began to melt, and he thought he might be on the verge, the very brink, of breaking down. His little boy would see him blub. The boy would see the father blub. He'd sit there, nibbling guava fruit, and watch his gutless father blub.

'It did occur to me,' he said, 'a year or two ago. I saw him lying fast asleep and it came to me, quite suddenly, quite brutally, that he might not be my own.'

'That must have been a somewhat shrivelling thought.'

'It was,' Max agreed. 'And elegantly put, if I may say so. But now I see the likeness more and more. Sometimes it's as if I'm staring in a mirror. I look at him, and hear that shrill and piping voice, and remember the me that I left behind. And back it comes again, the complete and total pointlessness, the shitty insignificance, of childhood.'

Bruno raised a quizzical eyebrow.

'Do I detect a certain bitterness, old son? A

certain lack of *joie de vivre*, in the memory department? Because I hope you don't intend to whine, I hope you don't intend to whinge, for every time you do, every time you start to pout and begin to wallow in your past, I get a pain' – he touched his lower belly – 'right here.'

'You wouldn't agree then?'

'Evidently not. I recall things rather differently, in fact. I'd have said that they were good days, when we were lads.'

'Were they? That's nice for you,' Max said. 'That's really, incredibly nice for you. Mine were rather bad days, you see, and that's why I try to compensate for my boyhood days with my manhood days, which is only fair, I would have thought.'

He rubbed condensation from the window, and peered into the garden. It seemed excessively unkempt, for an owner so fastidious. The shrubs were looking ragged, and the grass was far too long, and the whole effect was rather inappropriate. Max hardly ever touched it, nor had he ever learned to give his trust to experts. (Aside from all the usual fears of men with sharpened implements, strong-armed types with spades and rusty shears, he couldn't bear the thought that they might bury something nameless in the earth, inter some rotting corpse beneath his grass, and creep about in smelly dungarees, and leer at him.)

'I look at Sam,' he murmured, 'and I see that pink and baby face – completely round, completely unprotected – and it makes me want to hurt him, sometimes.'

He watched a brownish bird, which might have been a sparrow, flex its leg and pluck an earthworm from the grass.

'I never do, though. One doesn't do that to one's kids,' he said, 'in Little Venice.'

He knew he had this need to tell it all to Bruno, to confide his darkest thoughts and go down on his knees and make confession of his sins, before he took that arrogance, that jutting pride, that oriental root and core inside his mouth, and quietly sucked it dry. For Bruno surely was the Devil, and Max's penance was to suck the Devil's dick, to guzzle at the fountain of his ever-grinning houseguest.

'If he weren't mine,' he pointed out, 'I wouldn't want to hurt him.'

A fairly clinching argument, when all was said and done. Bruno peeled a piece of loose tobacco off his lower lip. It was time to comfort Max. Time to nurture and encourage him.

'I'm only joking. I know he's yours. You did it by yourself, and I salute you. It's the miracle of creation, as they say. But one thing's always bothered me . . .'

He began to look perplexed. A furrow split the Bruno-brow.

'Just explain to me, explain it, if you can, why even gutless men can get a woman. For therein lies the mystery, my fine, tumescent friend: that a man like you, a man such as yourself, can find a woman – a slag perhaps, but still a woman – and lay her down, and fill her up, and make a lad . . .'

He pulled a plate towards him.

'. . . that's what I'd call a miracle.'

And peering down expectantly, he added:

'These look rather scrumptious. Are they custard creams?'

22

Why does Bruno say these things?

He doesn't know. They seem to bubble out of him, almost uncontrolled. He sits there at the kitchen table, and decides that he'll be good for once. He'll behave, for once. He'll be nice to Max, and make him happy. For now, at least, since it makes a pleasant change.

And then he cuts himself a generous slice of cake, and chews it fairly thoughtfully, and when he's swallowed all the crumbs, and washed it down with lemonade, he lets his mouth sag open and out pops something rancid. He parts his Bruno lips and out pops something that a guest like him should never say to a host like that. The gall of it. The total cheek. Bruno being reckless yet again.

For even though he's seen the writing on the

wall, the 'BRUNO OUT!' that someone sprayed on to the wall, the starkly simple message on the creamy stucco wall, he knows it isn't meant for him, he knows that paint-sprayed messages are never meant for him, that vulgar exhortations are never aimed at him.

But still, he thought. And yet, he added. The Bruno-Outness of the words was quite intriguing. The newboy rolled the phrase around his mouth, acknowledging the resonance, the near-poetic brevity. It must have been another Bruno, some frankly rather lesser Bruno, some wretch who'd doubtless caused offence, some upstart who would have to leave.

Such things occurred, from time to time. Not frequently, but now and then. Even in a place like Little Venice, even in a part of town where pillar-fronted buildings soared above the water, and cultivated types did cultivated things behind their stripped and painted shutters, it wouldn't be unheard of for a Bruno to depart. Not quite an everyday event, but not unheard of, either.

So he wondered who he was, this one they didn't want, this other one who'd had the gall to use his name, this Bruno who would shortly be pushed out. For even though his tongue is honed and razored like a blade, and he's trained his mind to analyse the most elusive concepts, he hasn't got the skill to read the signs, he lacks the basic intuition that could save him.

He's performing in his private circus, blindfold high up on the wire, and he doesn't know it yet, it hasn't yet impinged upon his quietly throbbing brain, but soon he'll slip, and fall, and plummet down. He'll miss his step, and lose his grip, and thud into the ground. Decreed by blood and destiny, Bruno's due to take a plunge.

It's nothing new. It happens, now and then. And perhaps the fact that Bruno's got a mouth on him, a big, insulting mouth from which he shoots his subtle barbs, his tender provocations, somehow mitigates what lies ahead. Perhaps the fact that Bruno lacks the self-preserving sense to pack his bags and leave, excuses all that happens when he stays.

In other words, it might be Bruno's fault. In fact it often is, they often say.

But all that still awaits him. Those special pleasures of the flesh are yet to come. Meanwhile he's relaxing at the table. Living for the current, precious moment. Eating buttered scones and baiting Max.

23

The conversation of the adults, disturbing though it was, began to peter out. The afternoon was drifting on, and the plates were nearly empty.

Max watched the houseguest clamp a pair of pliers around a walnut. A sudden, whiplash crack, and a jagged piece of shell bounced high into the air. Bruno gave a little sigh of pleasure, a soft yet manly exhalation of contentment, and raised his curly head and smiled across at Max, who knew by heart the newboy's repertoire of muted gasps and moans, his modest grunts of satisfaction.

'Do you think she'll come down later?'

Max shook his head.

'She can't quite manage it, today. Not both of us, she says. Not you and me together, as it were. In fact not even one of us, or so she claims.'

He observed how Bruno slipped the creamy nut between his teeth, was conscious that he closed his jaws and began to slowly masticate.

'She says she's very sorry.'

Give the little girl her due. She knew what was expected. She knew she'd let them down.

'She seemed to be contrite.'

He watched as Bruno's mandibles worked up and down. He watched him sit and chew, and realised that he barely made a sound. He ate so well, Max thought. Such elegance, he thought. So inoffensive, when he eats. No slap of lip on lip, he thought, resentfully.

'She said she'll try to make it up to us. Another day, she said.'

The newboy flicked his eyes towards the child.

'Some other time, perhaps . . . ?'

'She said so, yes.'

Bruno nodded briefly. That's fair enough, he thought. She couldn't always be on tap. Not every day. Not every single hour. So it was really fair enough, he thought. But did she give a reason?

'Did she give a reason?'

Max felt the slightest bit uncomfortable. The merest hint of pained distaste would perhaps be more precise. Not quite disgust, but something fairly close.

'I'm afraid that something's *happened* to her. Something rather gross, to be exact.'

Bruno's head jerked up, his blood began to pump and flow, his senses quickened at the news, and he felt his interest sharply rising.

'She's had what might be termed a mishap of an unexpected nature.'

Bruno swallowed shards of nut, and leaned towards his generous host, and murmured, *sotto voce*:

'Dare one wonder if it's serious?'

(The hopefulness with which he asked, the unselfconscious appetite.)

'She seems to think so. She seems to find it altogether quite alarming.'

'But then she's always been alarmist.'

Bruno mulled it over in his head, this rather novel situation and all its possibilities. Something gross had happened to their girl. Something so completely beastly that Max could barely bring himself to speak of it, and Max could bring himself to speak of almost anything.

The newboy tried to conjure up what it might be, he briefly shut his eyes and allowed himself to contemplate, indulged himself in visions of tormented female types. Oh bliss, he thought, oh decadence, and felt the soft and wrinkled skin, the talcumed flesh between his legs, begin to tighten.

'Might she be in pain?'

'That's fairly likely,' Max replied. 'Discomfort, at the very least, but pain is also possible. Not exactly *agony*, but aches and throbs and inflammations.'

He grimaced slightly, hunched his narrow shoulders, and slipped his hands between his knees.

'I'm afraid she's got her you-know-what.'

'You mean she's . . . ?'

'Yes,' Max said. 'She is.'

He sniffed, but made no sound. Noiselessly, he mouthed the word, that dreaded word so redolent of loathsome smells and substances, effusions that they didn't care to think about. They shuddered at the recollection, and their manly gorges rose. Thank God, they thought, we don't do that. Whatever else we do, they thought, we don't do things like that.

Bruno tried to sound concerned. He tried to make a little show of empathy. (How could she bear it, he was thinking. How could she be so *physical*?)

'I suppose it's not her fault,' he said. 'As such.'

Un*clean*, he nearly screamed.

'There's very little one can do,' Max said. 'They happen to her, now and then.'

'You mean she gets them fairly often?'

'Periodically, or so she says.'

'And don't they bother her.'

'One gathers that she's not too keen. She's really not too partial.'

'Any reason, in particular?'

'They make her bleed.'

'But so do we.'

'That's very true.'

'And she does like us.'

'She does.'

They sat there, round the kitchen table, endeavouring to banish from their minds all rank and noxious things: the whiff of curdled juices, the brownish marks which spread and dried, the stained, discoloured linen sheets. The mess of it. The total pong.

The light was fading fast by now. Dusk came creeping up and traffic sounds were floating in the distance. Max leaned across and flicked a switch, and a yellow glow caressed them both. It soothed their ragged nerves and made their hatred leak away, until they almost purred with mutual understanding, until they sat and almost ached with mutual comprehension, until they felt quite mellow in the yellow.

Sam was drinking something sticky from a

cup. He was slurping quite disarmingly, licking greasy lips and producing smothered burps.

'I'm four,' he said, to no one in particular.

Bruno pulled a face.

'I've been four,' he pointed out. 'It's no big deal.'

Max watched his only child, the single, breathing product of his loins, and thanked his pagan gods he'd never had another. The very thought of it appalled him, made him weak with self-disgust. He shuddered when he realised that he'd almost given way, allowed himself to be entrapped by those who clung, and puked, and made demands. He'd almost been sucked down, immersed in domesticity, been feminised into a life of fatalistic dreariness, of foul, disgusting decency. The horror and the whininess, the reek of infant milkiness, the repulsively grotesque allure of playing happy families. The whole debased attraction of the sweet, seductive tedium.

It hadn't happened yet, but if it ever did, should he ever, by gross misfortune, by some perverted quirk of fate, become a kindly, caring, cunt of a man . . . let them bury him first, let them finish him off, let them dig a hole in peaty soil and shove him in, dead or not.

He placed his hand on Sammy's head. The skull felt pleasantly malleable, as if it were clay that had not quite set, and he could, were he only to press slightly harder, leave a thumb-shaped indentation in the boy's soft bone. He whispered into the velvet ear.

'I made you, Sam. Daddy did it, so don't deny it. One sticky, summer's night, when his slag was panting, and his head was spinning, and he shut his eyes, and held his breath, and stopped you trickling down his leg. Daddy made you, so be nice to him.'

He twisted the head around. He turned it with his hand, smoothly rotated it on the fragile neck, and stared at the blankly perfect face.

'Am I right, Sam? Tell me, Sammy, am I right?'

Sam began to laugh. The shrill and heartless sound of it. The son-of-slag began to laugh. His biscuit-flavoured breath came blowing from his mouth in milky gusts, his simple joy came scudding out, and Max was conscious of a sudden, dark, delightful urge to hit him on his smiling face and break the upturned, freckled nose.

'There's one thing on this earth I know . . .'

The freckled nose. The smiling face. The dark, delightful urge.

'I love kids,' he said, and kissed him hard. A hard and silent kiss. He kissed him hard on his downy cheek.

24

He'd always found the Bruno-smell disturbingly unwholesome. The Bruno-smell was one of sweat and cigarettes, alcohol and manly fluids. It settled in the room while he was there, and lingered when he'd gone. The smell alone, he realised, would have been enough. The Bruno-smell, that less than pleasant Bruno-smell, was cause enough. That she could even bear it, somehow only made it worse.

But soon be gone, he told himself. Soon be but a memory. He thought she'd probably take it well. She'd always been quite good like that. Surprisingly pragmatic, for one so Continental. Perhaps she'd wallow in a sulk, for a day or two. Compress her painted lips and turn her fine-boned face away. Perhaps she'd tie a plain black ribbon round her arm, and flaunt her vulgar grief at him. Perhaps she'd even turn him down, procrastinate until his courage wilted, and leave him standing in the hallway, all alone, if only for a day or two.

The thought of it, the very thought of how she'd tease him, what she'd do to keep him waiting, made him want her even more. He had a sudden, sharp nostalgia for the way things used to be, the sunlit days before it all went sour. He remembered how it was before his houseguest came and spoiled it all. A distant, golden age when the nights were long, and she was shyly grateful to be his and his alone. And the sense he'd had, the delicious sense he'd had, when pushing deep inside, of being faintly sullied.

One day she'd thank him for it. She'd come to him – all breasts and brimming gratitude – and thank you, Max, she'd say. (My pleasure, he'd reply.) I've sinned, she'd say, I've let you down. I've been a naughty girl. And then she'd take him by the hand, and lock the bathroom door, and help him teach her to be good.

The captivating thought of what he'd do to her. The endless possibilities: the shower-head, the toilet bowl, the water-heavy flannel. The soapiness of all her nooks and crannies. It made him weak to think of it, in a rampant kind of way.

Not too long to wait, at least, and then he'd

start again. He'd do it right, next time. With Bruno gone, he'd have a chance to get things right. He'd buy her things, and try to keep her happy. For underneath it all, no matter where they came from, they had a single need in common. There was a basic, female trait that all the sisters shared. He wouldn't have said he blamed them, for he was a non-judgmental man, but beneath the perfume and the pouting lay their beating, venal hearts. The bitches always wanted things. They measured him by what he gave, and what he gave was never quite enough.

She'd been the same. Even though she'd come from some forsaken patch of dirt, she shared the sisterhood's philosophy. Give me, Max. Just make me happy. Shower me with gifts. I'll make it worth your while, she'd say, and bend and seal the bargain.

Then Bruno came, with his handmade suits and broker's smile, and said: 'I'll have some of that. A bit of that will do me fine. Just a tiny bit, to while away the hours.'

And Max had shared the little that he had, the ungrateful little sow he had, and the brothers romped in the romper-room, and picked apart the spoils like brothers should.

Once Bruno had departed, she'd get over him. The doe-eyed coprophiliac would learn to cope without him, she'd learn to do without her daily dose of Willesden Green. Time would heal her open wound, and Max would take her in his arms, and hold her tight, and make her his once more. He ran a hand across his scalp and thought of how he'd comfort her. He loved to feel his shaven head, the reassuring viciousness of stubble on one's head. It was time he went head-first, impinged himself between her thighs, scrubbed the little scrubber with his skull.

It would teach her, he believed, a thing or two. And then he thought she wasn't one to learn. And then he thought he maybe shouldn't bother. But then he thought he'd like to do it anyway. To comfort her, if nothing else.

He'd just begun to fantasise, to picture in more detail how he'd shaft her with his cranium, when he heard a key slide in the lock. He knew it must be Bruno, for Bruno had a way with keys. A great unlocker, Bruno was. A thruster-in to rank among the best of them. He'd stick it in, and twist it round and release the catch. One day he'd simply ram it in. Another day he'd slide it in. No door was ever locked, to Bruno. He'd poke his polished tool inside the waiting space and turn it clockwise, sometimes anti-, and every lock would sigh and give.

And there the boy would be. Ensconced, once

more. With a single bound, he'd be inside. Don't mind me, he'd say. I'm only visiting, he'd say. Just passing quickly through. (The self-effacing Bruno grin. That stinking Bruno grin.)

The key turned in the lock, the door banged shut behind him, and he came into the room. Here he was, the lad himself, all supple self-assurance. So confident he seemed, as if he stepped inside by right, not just on sufferance. That was what was wrong, Max thought. That's the basic trouble with the Brunos of this world. As an act of grace, you let them visit you at home and helped them to relax, but they always went too far, they always crossed the line. So now he had to repossess, foreclose on Bruno's loan, evict the boy and send him packing. There'd be a scene, of course. And Max detested scenes, of course. But he had to let him go.

'Surely not champagne?' Bruno was impressed, although he tried to keep it to himself. He did his best to leave the suburbs far behind.

'I'll do the honours, shall I?'

Such a happy chap, he was. Such a very cheerful fellow. He oozed and dripped with satisfaction, he effervesced with quietly ostentatious glee. The kind that often emanates from the young, and brave, and nightly sucked.

Two bottles of the very best. Max could be a

chum, he thought. He could really be a brick. Bruno pushed aside the silver-plated corkscrew, gripped the bottle by the hips, unpeeled the layered foil and popped the cork. Liquid bubbled out, and he filled a pair of crystal glasses, and handed one across. The host was looking strange, he noticed. Not glum, as such, but something near.

'You look distressed, old son. If I might be so bold.'

'Perturbed, I'd say.'

Bruno nodded, sympathetically.

'If something's bothering you, just let it out, just spit it out, just vomit up your angst on to the carpet.'

'The Chinese rug,' Max murmured, 'to be exact.'

He undid his collar and pulled his tie apart.

'I thought I'd wait until she got here. I thought I'd let the three of us assemble.'

He rolled up the sleeves of his brushed-cotton shirt.

'We few, I thought, we happy few.'

'You've been thinking, then.'

'It would seem so, yes.'

They sat and waited for the girl – the hub and focus of existence – to arrive. They waited for the common bond, the piece of shared and linking gristle, the thread of throbbing sinew, that joined them both together.

Bruno drained his glass. He ran his finger round the rim, and made it hum. He cleared his throat and smiled across at Max. Max scratched himself and smiled across at Bruno. They sat in faded velvet chairs, and scratched and hummed and smiled until they heard her buzzing at the door.

She buzzed three times, the refugee. In Max's modest estimation, once might well have been sufficient. A single and truncated buzz would do. But she'd been influenced by Bruno, she'd let herself be tainted by the houseguest, she'd gobbled on his Devil's dick and swallowed all his nourishment, and now she always kept her finger on the buzzer.

Max let her in, and led her through, and sat her on the sofa. Carefully, he stretched her out, he spread her on the cushions. She looked, he thought, quite ravishing.

She was wearing something new, he noted, some outfit that he hadn't seen before. An almost tasteful compilation of almost toning shades. Stiletto heels to almost match. But her face was unaware, the face was blank of comprehension. She had no sense of things unfolding. A profoundly senseless girl.

He moved across to the bay and glanced out

at the water. Fresh air, he thought, might be a help. Bending down, he flexed his knees, and pulled the centre-window up. It jammed, of course, as sashes often do, and he resolved to fix the cords next week, to rub them roughly down, to be a touch more liberal with his stock of candle-wax.

He turned to his guests.

'I thought it time to have a little chat,' he said. 'Some verbal intertwining, a bit of oral give and take. What might be termed a *conversazione*.'

The newboy poured himself another glass. He gave himself a decent measure, a fairly generous slug of vintage Little Venice.

'Something wrong?' he asked. 'A problem we could help you with?'

Max stared at him reflectively, as if to memorise the face, to tuck its dark, exotic features in his mental envelope, and lick the flap and stick it firmly down. He wasn't quite sure how to put it, how to help them comprehend his finer feelings. He wanted to convey the undiluted essence, the pure, untainted core of what he felt.

'I've been having problems with my id,' he said, 'and I thought it time to let you know.'

It was out, he thought. He'd cleansed himself.

'I've pandered to my baser urges, been a trifle self-indulgent . . .'

'And you think it's got to stop?' (Bruno, ever helpful.)

'. . . and I'd like you both to know I've had a ball. I wanted to apologise, in case you thought I'd gone too far, because to me,' Max said, 'to put myself at centre stage, for once, it seems appropriate to take it even further.'

He felt himself expand. He was floating in the air.

'The problem is,' he said, 'it's all become monotonous, of late. I've found it rather tedious. In short,' he shrugged, 'I'm bored.'

He paused, to check that they were listening, to ensure that they were following the narrative.

'And then, of course, one needs to satisfy one's other thing.'

'One's id thing . . .' Bruno prompted.

Max smiled at him.

'I knew you'd understand.'

'That's what friends are for.'

'I must admit I've often wondered.'

'Have you specific ideas in mind, or would you like suggestions from the floor?'

'I think you ought to know that I've been toying with certain images, of late.'

'Forbidden ones, I hope.'

'You can safely rest assured of that.'

Max gazed fondly at his guests. Soon they'd all be sitting down to eat, partaking of the forbidden fruit of his forbidden images, and even he, even Max, would have his chance to salivate.

He crooked his finger at the foreign person. Obediently, she rose. How dog-like she could be, he thought, how grateful to be kept and fed.

'Why don't you pop outside,' he said, 'for a little while. Try and be domesticated. Change the sheets, or clean the bath, you know the type of thing. Amuse yourself, why don't you.'

She didn't argue, merely scowled in Slavic fashion, and flounced, to their delight, outside. They heard her bang the bedroom door behind her. It brought them close, as it always did. She was their baby, their dribbling child, the single thing on earth that made them tolerate each other.

'Can't she stay?' the newboy asked.

'I'd rather not,' Max said. 'She's always in our interactions. They always feature you-know-who. She's a kind of itching presence, always there.'

'Like a herpe.'

Max looked relieved.

'Have you had them, too?'

'Not exactly, but I've read about them. One tends to read, from time to time.'

That figures, Max reflected, for Bruno often made a point of pursing prissy lips and slipping on a featherlight, before he got stuck in. He often made a show of taking namby-pamby pains to keep the germs at bay. Trust Bruno not to get diseases. Trust him to be infection-free. Not fair, he thought, no justice on this earth. A silent mental image sprang to mind: Bruno ailing, Bruno rotting, Bruno dying all alone . . .

Max blanked out all bewitching thoughts, all heavenly imaginings of decomposing younger men, and brought himself, though not without an effort, back to earth.

'I thought it better we should be alone,' Max said. 'On this very special day.'

Bruno waved his newly empty glass. He understood entirely. An hour or so of buddy-talk, before he went. A final measuring of assets, a weighing-up of gonads.

'Don't worry, Max. I packed last night.'

'Enthralling news.'

The newboy stretched, and rubbed his neck.

'Cleared out my room and made the bed.'

'Remarkable.'

They could hear her moving furniture behind the wall. Muffled noises wafted in, pointless thuds and shrieks of Continental rage.

'D'you think the two of you will manage it without me?'

'We'll have a go,' Max said. 'We'll do our best.'

'Which might not be the same.'

'Quite possibly. One can but try.'

Max stepped a little closer, although proximity offended him. To stand too near his houseguest made him feel so ill at ease. Nothing personal, he told himself, and he didn't want to give offence, but he found excessive closeness quite disturbing. Bruno must have felt it too, for he always seemed to look away. He always turned his head when Max stepped up too near.

'So this is it,' Max said.

Farewells, he knew, were not his forte.

Bruno merely smiled, and looked away. A brief and understated movement, which he hoped would barely register. He often had to do that, when Max was standing next to him, when he breathed patrician breath on him, exhaled a mite too deeply, and Bruno caught a whiff of ravaged gut, the faintest hint of ulceration. For Max was slowly putrefying, corroding from within, and Bruno often felt the need to glance away.

'She'll miss me, though,' he pointed out. 'Seems that I remind the girl of home.'

'Of course you do.'

Max stood a little more erect, almost at attention, almost on parade. Of course he did, he thought. Reminded her, that is.

'She looks at you, and small world, she

thinks. Fancy that, she thinks. Now there's a familiar sight, she thinks. I mean there must be one or two of you, back where she belongs. At least a sprinkling, wouldn't you say? A seasoning, so to speak. A few of you still wandering round. A handful that they overlooked.

'One clears them out, and back they come. That's frankly what one finds endearing. Resilient types, so very *keen*. And they do keep coming back, you see. Quite gluttons for it . . .'

'Just like her.'

'Precisely.'

Max felt the blood begin to pump, the warmth to flow, his root and core begin to swell.

'One has to admire them, one really does. Indeed, one often *aches* with admiration. And therein lies the nub, if you'll forgive the technicality. Therein lies the paradox, the eternal Bruno paradox, old chum.'

'Do tell . . .'

Max saw he'd captured Bruno's interest, and paused, for half a minute, to ensure he kept it. For Max was only human, and he relished being listened to, he relished being thought a raconteur. He waited till he'd milked the moment dry, until he'd reduced it to an empty husk, and then revealed the essence of the problem.

'It goes like this,' he said. 'On your personal, micro level, you're a hairy brute with big ideas.

But on your national, macro level, you've been feminised. You're ripe for shafting. An enticingly anal nation is how I'd put it, if I were really pushed.'

But Bruno merely grinned at him. That stinking Bruno grin.

'Shall I stay for dinner, then? Seeing as I'm here?'

'Better not,' Max said. 'Let's not prolong the parting.'

The newboy looked so clean, he thought. Even though he was so dirty, he had a way of looking clean. A trick he must have learned, some sleight-of-hand passed down through generations.

'It's time to say goodbye, Bruno.'

Max leaned a fraction forward. He touched his lips to the young man's cheek, was conscious of the razored jaw, and allowed himself a muted grunt, a small and perfect moan, a muffled sob of pleasure, as he pushed the hand that held the corkscrew in and up.

'Goodbye, Bruno.'

He twisted it, he screwed his friend, then pulled away, and left an inch of metal poking from the open belly.

Bruno sagged, and tried to stand, then fell against the marble hearth. The crack of unprotected cranium on black, Italian tile. She must have heard, Max thought. Staring down he wondered, for a fleeting moment, why he'd done it. Then recollection came, and he felt a need to explicate. It was the least, the very least, the boy deserved.

'It's not the chip, as such,' he said. 'It's the principle of the chip.'

Bruno on the floor, at last. Gushing on the floor. He'd taken him, the mocking guest who wouldn't leave, and put him on the floor. And every piece of excrement that Max had ever eaten, throughout his long and dung-filled life, was paid for in that single, shining moment.

'I did this,' he said, 'I brought you down to this,' he said, 'you prick, you dying prick, don't look at me like that.'

The houseguest blinked, from time to time, and tried to move his lips. He looks quite stunned, Max thought, as well he should. He bent to pull the corkscrew out, but so deeply was it wedged, so thoroughly embedded, that he had to place a knee on Bruno's chest and heave, for twenty seconds, before he could release it. The ripping sound it made was one he'd never heard before. A strange, seductive sound, evocative of nothing. The sound was just itself: the sound of Bruno being gently ripped apart. Max gazed at him and shook his head.

'You don't look well,' he said. 'You're bleeding bad.'

He wiped the dripping spiral on the sleeve of Bruno's jacket.

'But then again, you always were a bleeder.'

The Bruno-stain was spreading on the carpet, while the boy himself, the object of the exercise, had clamped his hands across his unzipped abdomen, as if thereby to hold the sides together. Noises of an undetermined nature issued from his mouth, groans and sobs and little whimpers. Max felt moved, and almost tender, when he realised that he'd made his houseguest whimper.

'I'll admit I'm going to miss you. Bear in mind that you'll be missed, which frankly speaking can't be bad. We'll think of you, the girl and I. Tonight, perhaps. You're a much-loved man, old mate.'

He patted the glistening newboy brow.

'And I can't say fairer than that.'

Max stretched, and yawned, and lumbered to his feet.

'What you are experiencing now,' he explained, 'is what we term a moment of existential uncertainty. You are teetering on the brink of the great unknown, and the merest breeze, the slightest gust, could send you toppling over the edge.'

He touched the buttons of his fly, to check he'd done them up. He was feeling remarkably mellow, and he hoped it didn't show.

'You're ebbing, Bruno. Fading fast.'

He gave what he hoped was an encouraging smile.

'But not long now,' he promised. 'Nearly over now. We've almost finished, now,' he said, and picked up from the mantelpiece a thick and oblong bar, encased in waxy paper.

'The fact is, you've been saying things.'

The slow unpeeling of the wrapper.

'Making remarks that you shouldn't have made.'

The crumpling in the fist.

'Mouthing off, somewhat.'

The flicking to the floor.

'Shouldn't have done that, as it happens. Shouldn't have been so talkative. Your trouble is, you go too far. That's your fundamental trouble, and now I've got no choice.'

He gently moved his foot, he inched it forward, and nuzzled Bruno's sheet-white face with the tip of his calfskin shoe. He'd always wanted to nuzzle him, and he felt he did it rather well. Not without a certain empathy, all things considering. When he took it even further, and scraped his shoe on Bruno's cheek, and wiped the leather sole against the jutting

Bruno bone, he had a sense that they were somehow bonding, in a way they never had before.

But the houseguest had to concentrate. He had to make an effort. He had to try to understand what Max was going through.

'Are you listening, Bruno? Because I'm talking, Bruno.'

Max held the sculpted, pale-green slab beneath his nose, and sniffed, and pulled a face. A shade too sweet, perhaps. A shade plebeian.

'Because you made up all those lies, because you slandered one who cared, I'm going to have to wash your mouth out. Clean out all that Bruno-dirt that's swilling round in there.'

He stood beside the nearly-corpse, conscious of the unwrapped bar, the smoothness on his palm, the weight of it.

'I'm doing it for you-know-who, in case it crossed your mind to ask. He doesn't interest me, she said. Finish him, was what she said. Do it for me, Max, she said, and what the lady says, old Maxie does. For I like to please the ladies. I like to satisfy my ladies. I like to give them what they want. So bye-bye Bruno. All the best. Chin up, old mate.'

He squatted on the floor, beside the seeping man.

'I know you might imagine things look bleak,

but just remember that you've won a *moral* victory, and that's what counts,' Max said.

'It really does,' he emphasised, and pinched the nostrils shut, with thumb and index finger, and popped the bar of pale green soap into the suddenly open mouth. He knew he had to hurry, for Bruno might decide to faint, he might lose consciousness deliberately, to spite him.

'Please don't black out, just yet. Bear with me, if you can.'

He stood, and sighed, and pressed his aching back. Too old for this, he thought. It's more a young man's game. More suitable for brave young bloods. He heard a scuffling noise from somewhere in the hall. He held his breath and listened. Was that her outside? Has she got her uninvited ear pressed flat against the panelled door? And if she has, does he give a damn?

Max gazed down at the floor. Bruno looked quite drained, he thought. He was doubtless feeling gutted. A word of comfort might not go amiss, for he wasn't one to bear a grudge. So a moment of reflection seemed in order, a sharing of perception, a final squaring of accounts.

'I've often wondered why it is that certain types, certain sleek and chosen types – no inference intended – will always finish up like this. No matter what one does, they always have to make a scene. It always ends in tears.'

And having thus philosophised, he placed a single, well-shod foot on the stretched and slab-filled mouth.

'I hope you like my shoe,' he said. 'Bad boys often wear good shoes,' he said, and pressed down hard with the handmade sole of his bad-boy, calfskin shoe.

'Tea-time, Bruno. Eat your grandma.'

The smooth and perfumed bar slid over the tongue and into the throat, and Max watched, not unexcited, as his not quite former house-guest gently began to gag.

25

And what of Bruno?

What was Bruno feeling, as he fell? What insights forced their way inside his brain, what sudden, pin-sharp comprehension, as the four-inch metal spiral screwed itself beneath his skin? For Bruno also has a consciousness of pain when something sharp is thrust into his abdomen, and gouges out an unexpected hole. For Bruno also bleeds.

The cosmic disbelief came first, a nano-second's questioning of what had just occurred, a fleeting non-acceptance of reality. This can't be right. It's surely some mistake. Not Max, he thought. Not this, he thought. Not me.

But then he sagged, and tried to stand, and fell against the hearth, and heard the crack of someone's unprotected cranium. (The fireplace, he recalled, was of flecked and polished granite. He used to gaze at it admiringly, for like many from the less beguiling suburbs, he'd always been quite envious of understated wealth.)

But enough of that, he told himself. Enough of sycophantic longings, when I'm bleeding. He turned his head and saw the gaps between the tiles, and in the gaps a slightly darker sediment, composed of grease and biscuit crumbs. How very sad. How very gross. How absolutely unappealing. Must tell Max. He ought to know.

His mouth felt dry. Completely parched. As if a dentist's suction-tube had sucked out all the fluid. He found he couldn't swallow. Must be that champagne, he thought. Always dries you out. Remember not to swill it down, the next time that it's offered.

A coughing spasm shook him, and he brought up bitter liquid from some bursting, inner pool. That's more like it, he exulted, as the wetness filled his mouth, and overflowed, and dripped on to the floor.

Max was kneeling next to him, breathing quite erratically, pulling out the thing he'd pushed inside.

Hello Max, he tried to say. Maxie-boy, he nearly added. Who'd've thought it, me and you, and ending up like this? Small world, he didn't quite conclude. Small fucking world.

It's shining in my face. The bastard light's too bright. Should I ask him, and if I ask him, if I ask politely, will he turn it down? He spread his fingers on the wound and felt his essence seeping out. He wasn't gushing to an end, just slowly seeping. Not with a bang, but whimpering.

Should have gone. Should have listened when he said I had to go. Should have packed my bags and left, before he pulled the drawbridge up. The liquid in his mouth began to trickle down his throat, then changed its course and flooded up again. Max was softly murmuring, gently comforting, inserting something smooth between his teeth and wedging them apart.

He watched his host get up and press his no doubt aching back. He's much too old for this, he thought. It's more a young man's game. More a game for brave young bloods. He heard a noise outside. Was she in the corridor? Has she got her uninvited ear pressed flat against the panelling? And would Max give a damn?

The footsteps went away, then came back down the hall. She stopped and listened, quietly lurking, by the door. The tantalizing sound of someone stateless by the door.

It's her, he screamed, it's really her. She'd come to save him. Girly to the rescue, dressed in almost toning shades. Don't be silly Max, she'd say. A joke's a joke, she'd say, but this has gone too far. Apologise, and let me put a plaster on. Then Max would do as he was told, and step aside, and watch her bend and touch and make it better. Bruno played the little scene inside his head. He let his mental drama run, applauding with appalled relief.

Redemption was about to come. It was walking up the corridor, then paused, and coughed, and stepped inside the room. It wore an almost tasteful compilation of almost toning shades, and looked, he thought, quite ravishing.

Redemption on stiletto heels. It stared at him and touched itself. It sniggered, quite endearingly, and on its face a look of such profound delight, such near-orgasmic joy, such relish at the sight of him.

So this is what she likes, he thought. So now I know.

26

She assumed, at first, that they were just pretending, indulging in a bit of rough and tumble, some laddish game they'd teach her later on. But when she stepped inside the room and saw that one was grinning, the other seeping, she realised that they'd intermingled on their own, they'd played the game without her.

She saw the well-shod foot on Bruno's face. Max was strangely altered, indefinably different, as if he'd sucked out Bruno's sap, that Bruno-liquid they knew and loved, and made it all his own. He looked so large, she thought, beside the shrivelled form, the squeezed and empty husk. Max suddenly looked so huge, she thought, and even when he breathed, his breath seemed somehow sweeter.

'And then there were two,' he said.

He moved towards her, treading dark brown footprints into the Chinese rug. He came right up and stopped an inch or two in front of her, dripping drops of houseguest from his fingers. Grotesque, she thought. If not obscene. He should have had the decency to wash his hands, to rinse them clean before he made demands. She hoped he wouldn't make her wrap her mouth around his thumb. There was a time and place for everything, and she hoped he'd understand it if she'd rather not, for now.

The hygiene aspect worried her. She'd often wondered how a man like Max, a well-bred man of style and cultivation, a man of such complete and rare refinement, could bear to have such fingernails. How come a man like that could bear to see the grime encrusted round the rims? It wasn't right, she thought, the griminess of Max's nails. It shouldn't be allowed.

If she kept quite still, she told herself, he might decide to poke her with his dirty finger, he'd stick his filthy nail inside, he'd make a thoughtful gift of grime. If she didn't move, she told herself, it might occur to him, just might, she felt, to do an awful, truly dreadful, truly, truly, thing like that. He might decide to do it, if she managed not to move. So she stood and watched him dripping newboy on the floor, and she managed not to move.

He held her face between his hands, and tilted it to catch the light, and pressed his open mouth on hers. He kissed her with his open mouth, and cupped her glowing face, and smeared it with his hands. He pressed his urgent mouth against her face, and all the time the noise, the farmyard snorts, the little grunts of joy that pushed out from his lips, and trickled down his chin, and seemed to fill the room. He loved the heap of dirt he'd made. He daubed himself with all the dung, and smeared her smiling face so she could share it too.

'I did that,' he said.

His bright, unblinking eyes.

'I brought him down to that.'

He held her close. He hugged her tight.

'One doesn't want to brag, but it was me.'

Max observed the former guest. The pool in which he lay looked almost blackish in the light. The final escalation, necessarily accomplished. He felt a jolt of lurching glee, because he'd done the final deed, he'd put the newboy on the floor. He'd jammed the laughing Bruno-mouth, and laid him on the floor. And every piece of shit that Max had ever eaten, throughout his long and shit-filled life, was paid for in that incandescent moment.

He cupped his hand around her rump, could feel its warmth and readiness. The peach, he thought. The waiting cleft. All his again. In rightful ownership, once more. Back where it belonged.

'See this, old mate?'

He pinched the newly-reclaimed rump until he'd made her squeal out loud, then took a bigger lump of flesh, a hunk of unprotesting buttock, and twisted it again, with quite uncalled-for venom.

'This is what one gets for working hard. This is what one's money buys.'

But Bruno was oblivious. Max had won her back at last, and Bruno hadn't even noticed. The piece of selfish putrefaction couldn't even care. Max quietly cursed himself for being such a fool. He should have let him linger, he should have brought the girl in sooner, done disgusting things to her, before he'd finished off the newboy. It was his tenderness, he told himself. His tender, beating heart had let him down again.

When he shoved the girl away from him, she nearly slipped, she nearly lost her balance, she very nearly stumbled. It pleased him, quite excessively. He felt immense with pleasure. As if he'd somehow grown, as if he'd found completion. He loved to see her stumble. From this day forth, he'd be all grace and flow and beauty, and she would stumble after him. No Bruno, anymore, to interfere. The mollifying thought of being rather beastly. He could do the things he liked, without a newboy looking on. He gently slapped her on the still-unparted peachiness.

'Better have a wash,' he said. 'Pop outside and have a scrub. I think he might have had diseases, and you've got it on your face. Better rinse it all away.'

'I don't mind,' she promised. 'It's all the same to me,' she said, smeared with Bruno-succulence.

'Just scrub it off,' he said. 'I like it when you're clean.'

She stepped across the prone though not yet rigid form that lay, with some panache, beside the hearth. She walked out through the door, and down the hallway, and went inside the bathroom. She peeled off all her nearly-toning clothes. She climbed inside the cubicle, and slid the glass partition shut, and pressed the switch, and turned the knobs, and let the water from the shower power down. It stung her skin, and made her gasp, but washed away the grime. If nothing else, it made her clean, prepared her for the task to come. She stood directly underneath the flow, threw back her head, and rinsed the filth away.

For Max, she thought, for such as Max, one always has to suffer. She'd never be a mucky girl, the kind she saw down Edgware Road, the kind a Max just couldn't bear. With the water from the power-shower jetting on her skin, she swore she'd do her very best to please him. She wanted to be clean for him, if that was where his pleasure lay.

The steam became more dense. It swirled inside the cubicle, and thickened on the tiles. Water, steam and vapour in her mouth. She turned the pressure slightly down. That shaven head, she thought, as she stroked herself with shower-gel. That closely-shaven head, she thought. That stubble-covered scalp, she thought, and cleaned and scrubbed and stroked herself for shaven-headed Max.

The other one, the one who lay spread-eagled on the floor, the one whose final, mortal oozings filled the cracks between the tiles, that one she blotted from her mind. He wasn't someone that she cared to think about. She banished him entirely. Sent him into exile. Disappeared him from her consciousness.

But Max, she thought, her brave and reckless Max, she thought, and smoothed her foreign skin with scented cream. She spread the gel on both her palms, and covered all her choicer parts with foam.

She sensed the door slide open, more than heard it. She guessed he stood behind her, more than felt it. She saw his blue-veined arm snake out. It touched the left-hand knob and turned it anti-clockwise. Damp and steam built up again. He was standing close behind her. The water that came jetting from above began to fill her mouth. So hot he'd made it. Almost scalding. He positioned her beneath the shower-head. He moved her smoothly underneath, as the water from the shower powered down.

She was the focus of his life, the true and beating core of all he was, the sun that he revolved around. She felt him bend and kiss her neck. He murmured something brutal in her ear. He slipped an arm around her waist, and pulled her back against his groin, then turned the pressure down, because he didn't want to burn her, he didn't want to scald her prematurely. She knew it meant he really cared, and felt him slowly push inside the unresisting space, the pure and grime-free peachiness, she'd opened just for him.

27

Life had proved too burdensome, for Bruno. He'd been and gone and was no more, and not a whiff remained.

His end had been quite sudden, though not entirely unexpected, for he'd always been a mortal kind of man. Max, of course, had seen it coming, and even visitors from overseas, state-less persons passing through, freely-trickling foreign types consumed with self-regard, had noticed certain passions building up.

Only Bruno, being Bruno, hadn't guessed.

They felt quite fond of him, in retrospect. Now he wasn't there, they valued him enor-mously. But they didn't like to say his name. They rarely mentioned him in conversation. In referential terms, he wasn't very prominent. (They made allusions, now and then, but it didn't feel quite right, to pronounce the Bruno-word. The Bruno-word was better left unsaid.)

They missed the boy, of course, but they managed not to show it. They didn't let it get them down. They kept the anguish to themselves. Given what they'd suffered, the unrelenting trauma, they came through it all remarkably. They survived with sensibilities intact. In a word, they coped.

None the less, despite himself, Max felt, from time to time, the barest twinge of mild regret, a suggestion of a scruple, a consciousness of having been impulsive. He didn't feel remorse, as such. He wouldn't put it *quite* like that. It was more a kind of sadness, a sense of having somehow failed, of being forced to act against his nature.

'I'd describe it as an accident,' he said.

He felt he ought to make it plain. Clarity was called for.

'Not my fault at all,' he added.

It was a chilly autumn evening, and the two of them, just him and her, were lounging in the bay. They'd spent the intervening weeks becoming close again, commingling in corrupt and varied ways, and now they sat, exchanging insights, in the gloom.

'It's all a lie,' he said. 'A huge, tenacious lie.'

A rumour spread by malcontents, a rank and

scummy libel, a dirty, filthy defamation, for he'd
never meant to rip the boy, he'd never meant to
skewer him, he'd never meant to terminate, so
totally. These things happen, now and then.
Just can't be helped. The cut and thrust of daily
life. (And anyway, the little shit provoked him.)

'He asked for it,' Max pointed out.

'Demanded it.'

'Quite brazen, in the way he begged.'

'Forget it, then.'

She soothed him with her gentle smile. She
wiped away the doubt. Tranquillity descended,
and he felt his muscles slowly loosen, the tension-headache ebb away. So good, she was. So
comforting. So milk of human kindness.

Not only did she not accuse, she seemed to
empathise completely. She understood that
things occur, from time to time. She knew that
one can entertain one's guest, while quaffing
fairly good champagne and making random
conversation, and suddenly, quite fluidly, one's
pushed the corkscrew in and up, one's been a
rather awful beast, one's made an accidental slit
in someone's lower abdomen. Her virtue was
she knew all that. A very knowing girl.

He idly sniffed the air, and noticed that the
room smelled damp, a mustiness that seemed to
come from just behind the balcony. He hoped
the gutter wasn't leaking. Gutter-trouble was

something he could well avoid. The expense alone, he thought, the total inconvenience. The labourers he'd have to hire, the noise they'd make, the mess they'd leave, the way they'd try to finger what was female.

'My single lapse,' he said. 'My fall from grace.'

'He goaded you.'

'He drove me on.'

'He had to learn the hard way. You had to teach him what was what.'

'I suppose you're right.' The shrug, the heart-felt sigh. 'Someone had to do it.'

The light was fading fast, by now, and he squinted down towards the road. The man who owned the orange barge (the barge whose portholes beckoned so enticingly), was walking up and down the deck, hosing off the dreck of city life. Max watched him stepping over coils of unused rope, disjointed and supremely urban in his movements, as if he were aware that those who might be watching him, who might be sitting with their lady-friends, spying from their windows, looking down from slightly musty drawing-rooms, would do it more convincingly.

'The canal's infected, actually. Don't know if I mentioned it, but the water's got bacteria.'

Max willed the man to slip and topple overboard. He ached for him to do the decent thing.

'It's full of microbes.'

'Down below?'

'Germs and bugs and viruses.'

The slightly furrowed brow as he remembered.

'Weil's Disease, to be precise. Caused by rats who urinate. They like to do it while they swim, and frankly, who can blame them?'

'So if I bathed in it, I'd get a rash?'

'You'd catch your death, my love. So better not, I'd have to say. Better keep your panties on.'

Which prompted her to ask:

'Did you hide him, by the way?'

(The death-word might have been the cue. She was quick like that. Quite fleet of mind.)

'Because I looked in all the cupboards, and I emptied all the drawers, and I couldn't find him anywhere. I suppose you've stored him in the attic . . .'

She always had to needle him, encourage him to further acts. But he found it quite endearing, so he often let her prattle on, he often let her verbalise.

'I hope you haven't been upstairs.'

He watched the man rewind the hose and haul it to the stern.

'For if you have, if you've poked around inside my loft, I'll take you to the water's edge and shove your face inside.'

She curled up in the seat. She rearranged her hem and gently smoothed it down. The germs, she thought. The rat-borne bugs. She felt completely cherished.

'You'd do a thing like that,' she purred, 'for me?'

'One aims to please,' he said. 'One does one's best to satisfy.'

The streetlamps flickered on, and he mellowed in the yellow. Sitting by the window-ledge, he mourned the dear departed. He ruminated manfully. Half-slumbering, he thought of him, he brought the memories to mind. With unrequited yearning, with moist and wistful lassitude, with his hands between his parted thighs, he indulged in rumination.

'Are you happy, now?' he murmured.

'I am,' she said.

'Me too,' he agreed.

All gone, he thought. All irritants removed. The necessary dénouement: him and her alone again. But such a shame for Bruno.

'He's not upstairs,' Max said, at last, for he knew she liked to keep informed, she liked to keep abreast of what transpired.

'Not in the house at all. I spread him out a while ago. Divided him, and wrapped him up, and put the bits in plastic bags.'

'Did you leave him somewhere smart?'

He frowned as he recalled.

'A token piece, I think, by Chelsea Bridge, but most of him in Holland Park, and the rest in Maida Vale.'

(Good addresses one and all.)

'He's finally ubiquitous. He always thought he'd be a presence in the city. Now everywhere you'd care to look, there's a little piece of Bruno.'

'You said his name.'

'I did.'

He licked his reckless lips.

'One tends to, on occasion.'

They heard the buzzer in the hall, and Max was up and moving fast. For one so firmly middle-aged, he was moving very fast.

'Expecting someone round for dinner?'

Reluctantly, she followed him. It seemed the chummy little tête-à-tête, the exchange of recent news, the pleasures of their mutual cogitation, were temporarily curtailed.

'Someone I might know?'

She trailed him down the corridor.

'Some relative, perhaps?'

She watched him striding on ahead. Not languid, any more. As if he had some higher purpose, a better life ahead of him. She watched him moving swiftly down the hall, then slipping back the bolt, and swinging back the door, and shaking hands with someone dressed in black.

Someone rather young, and rather dark, and rather unfamiliar.

She watched the person step inside, and glance at her – or stare, to be exact – then slowly look away. Max led him down the hall. They seemed to be acquainted, in a casual sort of way. (A business friendship, possibly.)

'Before it slips my mind . . .' Max said, stopping right in front of her, '. . . and just to set you at your ease, in case you might have wondered . . .'

His face. His brutal, blissful, Maxie face. The heat of him. The stiffening. The bleak, unblinking eyes. She felt enclosed, contained, immensely grateful. Trepidations, and other moist sensations.

He propelled her gently forward, until he'd made her shake the hand, until he'd made her press the flesh, until he'd made her softly touch the unsuspecting newboy.

'This is Daniel,' he intoned. 'Daniel, this is her.'

He watched them interacting. Skin to fragrant skin. The bitch, he thought. The luscious bitch. He wiped saliva from his mouth, and murmured in her ear.

'I've told him all about you.'

Speaking softly, grinning hugely.

'I think he'd like to play the game.'